ALL BECAUSE OF YOU

"Vanessa, I asked you to leave the detective work to me. You didn't, so I had to make sure you didn't get hurt in the process."

"Then I guess I should thank you."

"You really want to thank me?"

Before she could respond, he captured her mouth again, this time kissing her with more passion and hunger than before.

Vanessa didn't want to protest or come to her senses. She wanted to go with the moment, to act on the lust and want that she felt for this man.

His beard was so close-shaven, it wasn't much more than a shadow. But she liked it. She liked the way he was so smooth. When he walked across the room, he looked so smooth. The way he'd grabbed her to kiss her, and how he held on to her was so smooth. His hands caressed her back, gently massaging her into a relaxed sensual state. . . .

ALL BECAUSE OF YOU

Bridget Anderson

BET Publications LLC
http://www.bet.com
http://www.arabesquebooks.com

ARABESQUE BOOKS are published by

BET Publications, LLC
c/o BET BOOKS
One BET Plaza
1900 W Place NE
Washington, DC 20018-1211

First Printing: May 2002
10 9 8 7 6 5 4 3 2 1

Printed in the United States of America

I'd like to dedicate this one to my family:
Margaret, James, Sr., James, Jr., and Terry.

One

"Man, what a lame way to check out."

"Yeah, I know. I can't believe he did it, either."

"What do you think made him do it?"

"Don't know. Thaw him Friday morning. He didn't theem depreshed or anything. He bounced in like alwayths. Nothing out of the ordinary."

The elevator doors opened and a flood of suits carrying laptop briefcases stepped off. The men watched as the doors closed and the elevator continued its climb upward. Nodding at a few coworkers, they waited casually for the next elevator going down.

"You know, his death reminds me of that guy last year."

"What guy?"

"The one from accounting . . . you remember, he offed himself last year."

"Oh, yeah. That guy."

The bell over the elevator announced more employees reporting to work. The doors opened again and Vanessa Benton stepped off.

The men smiled as her long legs walked by them in a suit with a short skirt. She looked professional and classy, as always.

"Morning, James, Ronnie. Going the wrong way,

aren't you guys?" she commented as she headed toward the double glass doors of Brightline, Inc.

Standing there, jaws dropped, they took a step back. Then Ronnie spoke up. "Morning. Just going down for thome coffee. You need anything?" His smile broadened as his lisp returned.

"No, thanks. I'll run down after I'm settled. See you later." She strutted into the office ready for the usual Monday-morning disasters.

After the elevator door closed, Ronnie commented, "She doesn't know."

James shook his head. "Somebody should have called her."

The office was quiet. Vanessa looked around at the empty cubicles scattered with family photos, little stress trinkets, and mounds of manila folders. She checked her watch. Seven-fifteen A.M.

After throwing her black-and-white striped tote bag on the desk, she noticed her message light was flashing, but she wasn't ready to start putting out fires just yet. She needed her morning dose of caffeine. After a thorough search of her purse produced no change, she stepped over to her partner's desk in the oversize cube they shared, and took a couple of quarters. Christopher kept a bowl for times like this.

She ran down to the cafeteria and returned with a cup of hot coffee with hazelnut creamer swimming in it. One look around and she realized there had to be a meeting going on. Maybe Jane, her boss, had called an emergency meeting, which was on the voice message Vanessa hadn't checked. Grabbing a steno pad and pencil, she ran around to the conference room where Jane held all her meetings.

She could see the people behind the beveled glass door as she approached. When she eased the door open, a few people looked back at her. Full house—she'd have to stand. She noticed a few eyes lower to the floor. Brenda, her lunch buddy, picked up a tissue and began wiping her eyes.

"That's all the information I have right now." Jane sounded tired and disappointed as she looked up at Vanessa.

A coworker reached over to gently caressed Vanessa's back. Why was he offering her comfort? She bet the company was laying off, or folding. After all, their financial problems weren't a secret. Things were so tight, the secretary was rationing out Post-its. Vanessa whispered to her coworker, "What happened?"

He whispered back, "You didn't hear?"

She shook her head and shrugged as Jane looked at her out of the corner of her eye. "No. I haven't checked my E-mails this morning."

"Well." He took a deep breath, then said, "The police found Christopher's body Saturday morning. He's dead."

Detective Eric Daniels sat behind his desk looking over the report of a possible suicide he'd just been assigned. Christopher Harris, thirty-one-year-old white male, found dead in downtown Atlanta outside of Dugan's Sports Bar. Dead from a single gunshot to the head. The cops on the scene declared the death a cut-and-dried suicide since the victim still held the gun.

During the interviews conducted over the weekend, people claimed the victim was depressed and complained a lot. However, the family wasn't buying the suicide.

Now, Eric's boss wanted the case closed before it reached the mayor's office.

The original detective on the case, Detective Archer, had been arrested earlier that morning for hitting a woman while driving in a drunken stupor. After numerous warnings he would finally spend time in a rehabilitation center for alcoholism. Or, so Eric had been informed. Now he had the job of closing the case.

"Hey, got a minute?" Detective Kenny Powell walked over to Eric's desk.

"Sure. What's up?"

Detective Powell had joined the force a couple of years after Eric. Because he chased all the pretty female recruits, he'd earned the nickname Lady-Killer. He was all right looking for a guy, Eric guessed. Women seemed to like that bald-head, earring-wearing look that Powell sported.

Powell walked over and sat in the seat next to Eric's desk. He dropped two folders on the desk. "What's going on around here?"

Eric shrugged. "What do you mean?"

"I've just been assigned two cases that look like the Keystone Kops wrote them up. I'll be weeks making sense of this stuff."

That same thought ran through Eric's mind as he read over his new case. He picked up Powell's file, glancing through it. "Looks like there's a lot of reassigning going on all of a sudden."

"Funny thing though, neither Butler nor Davis were given pieces of crap to work with. Man, I'm getting tired of this mess. How's a brother supposed to get a break, when they expect us to keep working miracles? I'm not Jesus."

"I feel you, man, but you know how things work around here." He set Powell's folders down, picking up his own. "I've got a cut-and-dried suicide case. What do they expect from me other than to close it out?"

"See, that's what I'm saying. Davis is investigating the death of some wealthy socialite in Buckhead. High-profile, just like I said." He sat back for a minute, looking defeated. Then he reached for his folders. "I'm looking at one homeless victim, and another gang banger. While I'm not saying these people aren't important, you get my drift. How's a guy gonna get a promotion with cases like these?"

"Torello got it in for you or something?"

"Not that I know of. I hope like hell he doesn't."

Eric gave Powell a curious look. There was more to his story than met the eye. "What's up, Powell? Not enough money to take care of the ladies?"

Powell suppressed an incriminating smile.

Eric knew then he'd hit the nail on the head. He also knew Powell had a habit of entertaining ladies of the night. "Man, you better slow down. You can't work miracles and chase women, too."

Powell stood to leave. "Don't believe everything you hear. I still want you to meet somebody. Remember that dancer I told you about?"

"I remember, and I'm still not interested."

"She's your type, man. Real classy, long legs, sharp wit, all-around type."

Eric leaned back in his chair, laughing. "How do you know my type?"

"Come on, we've been out together before. You're a leg men. I can see that. I'm telling you this is the woman for you."

"Powell, whatever you're selling, I'm not buying." The last thing he needed was one of Powell's hand-me-downs, or a prostitute. Powell spent too much time with shady ladies.

"Whatever, man. Look, if you change your mind, page me."

The carpet seemed to pull away beneath Vanessa's feet. She couldn't catch her breath, or stop the floor from moving. Maybe she misunderstood. How many Christophers worked there? She tried to focus and think. Of the three-hundred-some-odd employees, only one was named Christopher Harris.

Brenda caught the look on Vanessa's face as she rushed around the table. "Vanessa, are you all right?" She looked up into her eyes. "Somebody grab a chair," she yelled.

"What did he say?" Vanessa asked again, as her body was lowered into the seat.

"I know, girl. We're all in shock. I can't believe no one called to tell you." Pulling over another chair, Brenda sat next to her.

"What happened?" Vanessa asked, still confused and feeling dazed.

Her boss, Jane, stood to answer her question. "The police found Christopher sitting in his car Saturday morning. They think he killed himself."

Little droplets of pain trickled down Vanessa's leg as the cup trembled in her hand. Christopher kill himself? It didn't make sense. She couldn't even process the thought. Everyone around her moved in slow motion. She saw their lips moving, but couldn't hear them. A sick feeling ran all through her as the room began a slow spin.

"Somebody grab her coffee." A coworker noticed the coffee spilling onto her leg.

"I have to go." She jumped up from her seat maybe a little too fast. Her legs didn't want to cooperate. The last thing she remembered was losing her grip on the cup.

When Vanessa woke, she was at home on her couch. She moved to sit up, but a wave of nausea crept up, so she eased back down. The pain was still in her head, her stomach, all over her body like a cancer. The feeling was foreign to her. Her grief seemed a bit misplaced, or more as if a loved one had passed.

She could hear someone in the kitchen talking. She eased up again as Brenda walked into the room, holding the phone in her hand.

"Gotta run. She just woke up." Brenda turned off the phone and walked over to the love seat across from the couch.

"What happened?" Vanessa asked, holding her head in an attempt to stop the throbbing.

"You passed out. Jane suggested we bring you home." She set the phone on the coffee table.

"Who's we?"

"Ronnie from accounting helped me. He's out waiting in the car. You came to once. Then nodded back out. Scared the hell out of me."

"God, my head hurts." She leaned back on the couch, unable to believe she had to be carried home. "I can't believe I reacted this way. I've never passed out before."

Brenda leaned forward in her seat, resting her elbows on her thighs. "Me, neither. I'll stay with you for a while today if you want me to. I can have Ronnie come back for me later."

A tear rolled down Vanessa's cheek. "I don't understand. Chris was talking about going on vacation in a few weeks. Why would he kill himself?"

"Beats me." Brenda shrugged, and reached out for the

paper on the coffee table. "The newspaper called it a possible suicide, too. Here it is."

"No way." Vanessa grabbed the paper and read the small mention of a man found Saturday morning outside Dugan's Sports Bar. A possible suicide, according to the Fulton County police.

In utter disbelief, she dropped the paper on the table, shaking her head. Her pager went off at the same time. She grabbed the small black pager clipped to her belt.

"It's my sister, Betty." She set the pager on the coffee table and sat forward, stretching from her forced nap. "Brenda, thanks for bringing me home. I'm going to be okay now. I'll call Betty back."

Brenda stood. "Yeah, okay. I just wanted to make sure you were okay. Your car's in the driveway, and the keys are on the kitchen table."

"Thanks, Bren, and tell Jane I'll be in tomorrow morning." After walking Brenda out, Vanessa settled back on the couch and picked up the phone to call Betty.

"Hello, Williams residence." Betty always answered the phone sounding like a receptionist for the White House. Vanessa never understood why she had to be so formal all the time.

"You page me?"

"Yes. Where are you? I've been trying to reach you at work for hours. What's wrong? You sound strange."

Vanessa took a deep breath, then let out a loud sigh. When she opened her mouth to speak, her lip began to tremble. "Christopher's dead."

"Oh, my goodness. What happened?"

"I don't know. The police found him dead in his car Saturday morning."

"Just sitting in the car?"

"Yeah. I don't know any of the details yet. All I know is they're saying he committed suicide."

"Suicide! Was working with you that bad?" Betty let out a soft chuckle.

"Betty, that's not funny. I worked with that guy for over two years. We've closed out over one hundred accounts for Brightline. We were a great team."

"Vanessa, I'm so sorry. That was very insensitive of me. Are you okay?"

Between sniffles she answered, "Yes, I'm fine. I'd just like to know who killed my buddy."

Two

"Eric, she's here."

Detective Daniels stood and smoothed out his tie. This was his fifth—and last—interview of the day. "Thanks. Is she in the interview room?"

"Yes, and she looks a little scared."

He shook his head and grabbed the folder for the Christopher Harris case. "You'll be behind the two-way mirror, right?"

"Yes, sir, taking notes and listening to everything."

"Thanks, Mona." Eric knew he needed a female detective present; however, he liked to conduct his interviews alone.

As he walked down the hall, he glanced at the name on the interviewee sheet: Vanessa Benton. She shared work space with the victim, but hadn't been named in the theft charge. He'd see what she knew if anything about why Mr. Harris killed himself.

He opened the door, half expecting to see a frightened little woman sitting at the table picking her fingernails. Instead, he saw the backside of a curvaceous sexy woman who stood by the window talking on a cell phone. When he closed the door, she spun around. He admired her long shapely legs as she slid the phone into her purse.

"I'm sorry. I had to take that call." She stepped over to the long rectangle table with two old steel office chairs and sat down.

Eric put his tongue back in his mouth before clearing his throat. "No problem." He walked over to her and extended his hand.

"Thank you for coming down, Ms. Benton. I'm Detective Eric Daniels."

She shook his hand without smiling.

He sensed her turning up her nose at him as he sat down. She pouted her full lips as she sat there with a discontent look on her face. He dropped the folder on the table.

"How long will this take?" She raised her sleeve and checked her watch.

"I won't keep you long. Promise. I'm new to the case so I have a few questions I'd like to ask. Before we start, can I get you anything?" He smoothed down his tie again.

"No, thank you. I just want to get this over with." She gave him a quick smile that dropped into a smirk.

Eric took a deep breath, and reached for the small tape recorder in the middle of the table. She looked tense as she drummed her fingers on the arm of the chair.

"This interview is going to be taped—unless you have any objections?"

"No, go ahead." She shrugged.

He pushed the play button. "Okay, let's get started, shall we?" He opened the folder and picked up a pen from the desk.

Vanessa scooted her chair closer to the table. She crossed her arms and stared past him.

"For the record, could you state your name, date of birth, and place of residence?"

"You mean you don't already have that information in your notes?" She uncrossed her arms and pointed to the folder in front of him. "I'm sure you know everything about me already."

Not surprised, Eric dropped his pen and placed his

forearms on the table. He didn't feel like dealing with a smart ass this late in the day. Why was she being so difficult?

"Ms. Benton, I don't know if you've ever been in a police station before or not. And I don't know what your friends have told you about being interviewed, but you're not a suspect, so—"

"I've been in a police station before, Detective, and I know how you guys find out anything you want to know. So, you don't have to treat me like some scared little girl. Exactly what is it you want to know?"

Eric sat back in his seat, his elbows propped on the armrest. With his index finger, he stroked his mustache. Feisty—he liked that. Sure, he had her address, and he knew she was thirty-four years old. So, he'd have to change his approach with her.

"Okay, Ms. Benton. What was your relationship to Mr. Harris?"

"We worked together, that's all," she said absently.

"How well did you know him?"

"About as well as you can know a coworker."

"How long had you been working together?"

"For two years. We worked good together."

"Explain what you mean by that."

She let out a heavy sigh. "Our accounts. We have a good tracking system. We've closed everything out on time with minimal outstanding debt. Which is more than I can say for some of our peers."

"They have a lot of debt?"

She shrugged. "I suppose. Every year the company writes off what they can't collect. They never had to write off any of our accounts. We always collected the money. If I couldn't, he could."

"I see." He jotted down a few notes as he asked the next question. "When was the last time you saw Mr. Harris?"

She hesitated before answering. He looked up from his pad. The look on her face didn't match the sassy attitude she gave him.

"Last Friday. I worked until about five-thirty. He was there when I left. Christopher's not a morning person, so he comes in late and leaves late."

"Was there anything unusual about him that day? Was he nervous, upset, or anything like that?" He detected a wounded look in her eyes before she lowered her head.

Looking down, she traced small circles in the old wood table with her finger. "No, he was glad it was Friday just like everybody else."

"Did you know that Brightline had accused him of stealing from the company?"

Her head snapped up. "No. Stealing what?"

"Money."

"That's ridiculous. Who told you that?"

"The company filed charges Friday. And after talking with some of Mr. Harris's peers it seems you two were pretty close."

"We weren't that close."

"So, you didn't hang out after work Friday like you usually do?" He watched and waited for her facial expression to change.

She looked up, narrowing her eyes at him. "No, we don't *usually* hang out after work."

He picked up a sheet from the folder and read from it. " 'We sometimes go over to Jock and Jill's for drinks after work. Including Christopher and Vanessa.' " He looked up from the paper with a "got ya" grin on his face.

Vanessa sat up straight and leaned in her seat to slowly cross her legs. "Some of my coworkers go to Jock and Jill's to watch ball games. However, I don't usually go. I'm afraid somebody lied to you."

"I'll have to check that out," Eric said with a twist of his lips.

"Yes, you should." Vanessa looked down at her watch again. "Are we almost finished?"

"Yes. I just have a few more questions. A friend of Mr. Harris's told one of our officers he complained about money a lot. Do you know if he had any financial problems?"

"I wouldn't know. We didn't talk about money."

"But you cut checks for clients every day?"

"Accounting cuts checks. We processed the backup for payments, and authorized them. We never discussed personal finances. If you want that kind of information, I suggest you talk to his banker. I'm sure you can pull his bank records."

At first Eric chuckled, then lowered his head to pinch the bridge of his nose. She was too much. He pushed back from his seat and stretched out his legs.

"Ms. Benton, I can see you're rather distraught by your friend's passing, but being uncooperative with me won't help matters. I'm trying to help by getting as much information as I can, which means I have to interview all his friends. And since you spent about nine hours a day with him, you're high on my list."

She let out a deep sigh and held up one hand, palm out. "I'm sorry. I just don't like being here. I am upset about Christopher's death, but I can't tell you a lot about his personal life. He was a very private person who didn't talk about himself, or his money."

"I can respect that. I have one more question and you're free to leave. Did he have any enemies that you know of?"

She shook her head. "No, everybody liked Christopher. And he wouldn't hurt a flea."

"If you don't know much about him, how do you know that?"

"You just had to know him. He was a real mild-mannered guy. Never had a beef with anyone. He was good at minding his own business. He wasn't some nut running around trying to kill himself."

"So, you don't think he committed suicide?"

She slapped her hand against the table and rolled her eyes toward the ceiling, and exhaled. "No way. He had no reason to kill himself. He'd planned a vacation in a few weeks. Would somebody about to commit suicide plan a vacation?"

They stared at each other in silence for a few minutes.

"And by the way, that was more than one question."

Eric loved a good challenge. She had walked in there ready for a fight. Why, he didn't know.

"How about this? I've got another one for you. Do you know who he planned his vacation with?"

"He didn't say, and I didn't ask."

"Do you know if he owned a gun?"

"No, I don't."

He reached inside his jacket pocket for a business card. Flipping the card over, he scribbled down his home phone number before sliding the card across the table.

"Ms. Benton, if you think of anything else, please give me a call. Sometimes people remember things after a few weeks." He stood and pushed his chair back from the table.

She stood, pulling her purse up on her shoulder.

Eric reached out and offered his hand. "I'd like to thank you for your time today. And I'm sorry if I inconvenienced you in any way."

Vanessa read the back of the card while giving him a firm handshake and a cocky grin. "Detective Daniels, I came down here out of respect for my friend, because I want you to know somebody killed him. I don't know who, and I don't know why. But you're a cop. The who and why is your job, isn't it?"

Eric wanted to reach down and wrap his hands around her beautiful neck. She didn't hold back, that was for sure.

"Who, what, where, when and why—I'm working on it." He'd never let an interviewee get away with so much attitude before. Then again, he'd never been so attracted to an interviewee before, either. He focused on her sexy lips every time she moved her mouth.

"Are we finished?" she asked for the second time.

"Yes, and you're free to go." He walked over and opened the door for her. She strutted past, leaving the sweet smell of her perfume behind.

Eric stood in the doorway watching her backside as she strutted away. "Too bad I won't get to know her better," he said regretfully.

"She's tough," Mona commented as she approached.

"Yeah, I need another cup of coffee." Eric went to write up his statements.

"Girl, you're lucky he didn't lock your butt up on the spot. What did he say?" Betty handed Vanessa a hammer as they hung the living room curtains.

"He just looked at me and kept on asking those stupid questions with his fine self."

"He looked that good, huh?"

"Let me put it like this. It should be against the law for a man to look that good. He walked in in a smooth way and stood there a few seconds. Like he was giving me time to check him out. Then he started with the stupid questions."

"I thought you were eager to help Christopher. What happened?"

"It sounded to me like he thought I was in on something with Christopher. Like I knew more about him than I was telling. I also don't have fond memories of the police station. Detective Daniels should be out trying to find Christopher's killer instead of wasting time on standard questions." She hammered the nail against the wall with one loud tap.

"Ms. Know It All, how do you know what's standard and what's not?"

"Tony. Remember him? He was a cop."

"Oh, I'd almost forgotten about him—your 'Italian Stallion.' That's why you hate cops so much." Betty climbed down from the ladder.

"He was Italian, but he was no stallion. He was an abusive son of a—"

"Don't go there. Not in my house." Betty turned and pointed at Vanessa as she stepped off the ladder.

"God, Betty, I don't believe you. No smoking, no swearing, no, no. What else is it you don't like in your house?"

"No eating in the living room," Betty added.

"As if the place isn't already immaculate. You know, if you had a job, this place could hold a little dust like mine."

Betty laughed. "Girl, if I had a job, Harold would have a fit. I think he wants me barefoot and pregnant again."

"What? He wants another child?"

"Yep, that's what he said. We're discussing it."

"That's great. Where's my little nephew anyway?"

"He's with his daddy out of our way, so we can get these curtains hung."

"You know, big sis, I'm proud of you."

Betty stopped and smiled at her. "What for?"

"You have such a perfect little family. You have a devoted husband, a beautiful little boy, and this sharp four-bedroom house. You've got it all."

"Well, Harold works hard, and so do I. But I'm proud of you, too. Look how you've worked your way up at that company in such a short time. Daddy would have been so proud of you."

"Maybe after I get this promotion you can say that. I will have made it to management in two years."

"When will you know?"

"I'm not sure now. Things are kind of crazy at work. Somebody will have to pick up Christopher's work, but I hope they don't plan on giving it to me. I want that promotion."

"Well, whatever the outcome I'm sure you can handle it."

"I hope so." Vanessa knew Betty didn't understand how hard it was to scratch and claw your way up the corporate ladder. She hadn't worked outside the home since college.

Vanessa hadn't thought about Tony in years, until she walked into that police station. Old horrible memories came rushing back. Tony was her Mr. Right, until he raised his hand to her.

She first set eyes on him at an Atlanta Hawks basketball game. The minute she stepped out to find a rest room, she saw a tall, light olive-complexioned police officer standing across from the rest room smiling at her. His coal-black hair combed back, showed off his chiseled face, that cute dimple in his chin, and his cobalt eyes.

Trying not to trip over herself, or lose her bladder too soon, she smiled back and hurried into the ladies' room. When she exited, he was waiting outside the door. She got a better look at his rock-hard body, and she was so into muscles. After that day they became an item.

At first, she felt safe with Tony around. He treated her like a queen. He wined and dined her, brought her flowers, even took her on short weekend trips. She had no idea the average policeman didn't earn the kind of money he was spending. As soon as she found out where his money came from, she wanted out. However, he didn't want her to leave. She was his.

The first time he hit her, she ran home to her mother. The second time, she fought back. The third time, she called the police to have him arrested. That's when she learned how tight the bond was between officers.

A week after Christopher's funeral, personnel came by to clean off his desk. Before they took everything, Vanessa grabbed the little beanie toy he kept on his desk. Every time something upset him, he threw the little crab and listened to it say, "This place sucks." It was his stress reliever, and the secret to why he stayed so calm all the time. After they left, she returned it to his desk as a reminder. Aside from the crab, she had some of his work as a constant reminder. Her boss hadn't assigned anyone to pick up Christopher's workload. Nor had her promotion to in-house contracts come through yet.

"Girl, it's after five. You going to Jock and Jill's with us tonight?" Brenda leaned over the petition between their cubes.

Vanessa sighed, looking at the mound of folders. "I don't think I'll make it tonight." She thought about what the detective said, and wondered if Brenda told him about Jock and Jill's.

"I don't believe this. *You* miss a ball game. Girl, I know how much you love ball. And it's the Lakers vs. the Rockets. You don't want to miss this one."

"I'll get home in time to catch the second half."

"Is there anything I can help you with?" Brenda offered.

"No, don't worry about it. Go ahead, and have a good time for me, too."

"Come on, blow this Popsicle stand and come have a beer on me. I'll help you catch up tomorrow."

"I might take you up on that sometime, but not tonight."

"Brenda, come on, girl," another coworker called out from the end of the corridor.

"My money's on the Lakers. We'll discuss it tomorrow."

"Sorry, you're going to lose. The Rockets have got this one wrapped up. But I'll wait until tomorrow to brag. Look, don't you work too hard." She grabbed her purse and joined her friends.

"I'll try not to." Vanessa frowned at the mound of folders on the corner of her desk.

Four hours later, she called it quits. She locked her desk, and grabbed her purse and tote bag. Heading for the elevator she noticed that end of the hall was pitch-black. Only the lights on her side of the building were on. When she reached the copy room, she peeked inside. The control panel for all the lights was just inside the door.

She flicked the switch up and down several times, nothing happened. "Damn." She looked around to see if anybody else was in the office. She heard music coming from a few rows down. She took a few steps backward then turned around heading toward the music.

"Hello," she called out, hoping somebody would answer. When no one answered, she tried again. "Hello," she said louder this time.

The music grew louder as she walked down the aisle. When she reached the cube it was empty. Someone had left their radio playing.

"Shoot." She stomped her foot. She was a little afraid of walking down that dark hall. The side effect of too many scary movies, she reminded herself. She could take the stairs, but they were on the eighteenth floor and she wasn't about to climb down eighteen flights.

"Okay, you can do this," she told herself. She took a deep breath and dashed down the hall to the elevator. The moonlight glowing through the glass walls across from the elevator cast enough light for her to see the buttons. She pushed several times in quick unison, as if the elevator would show up faster.

"Come on, come on." She bounced around, and stopped when she heard a squeaking sound. Her heart jumped up into her throat. "What was that?"

Three

Everything was quiet. She hadn't come home from work yet. Large shrubs surrounded the backyard for privacy. Earlier that day he knocked out the streetlight, assuring even more privacy. Something crunched, so he stepped back and looked down at the remnants of a broken pot under his foot. Cursing under his breath, he sent pieces of pottery flying across the yard. As he approached the back deck, a smile slowly crept to his lips. "Oh, how feminine." The deck looked cozy and inviting with an old-fashioned white swing and what looked like hundreds of potted plants. A large table with an umbrella set on one side next to the barbecue grill.

He reached the back door and tried the knob. Locked, of course. Before sliding his hand into his jacket pocket, he took a quick look around—nothing but shrubs. Oh, how he loved privacy. He pulled out his trusty crowbar and gripped the doorknob again. With one swift pop he repeated a job he could do in his sleep. His full weight against the door only caused a faint rustle sound as the door opened. Not a sound. No alarm, no dog, nothing but the sweetness of silence. His favorite type of invitation.

He closed the door behind him and pulled out a small thin flashlight. He stood in the kitchen shining his light around the room. No dirty dishes, no mess. The room was spotless. He proceeded through the house to her office, not needing a map to scope it out.

Once inside, he made sure the blinds were closed. He shone the flashlight over the top of her desk. Next to a few envelopes was a small bowl of liquid. He picked up the bowl and smelled it. Water.

A stack of folders sat in the middle of the desk. He turned on the small desk lamp, pulled the chair back, took a seat, and started sifting through the piles.

After looking through about a third of the paperwork, a bright light shone past the window. He quickly turned off both lights. He'd never been caught, and he wouldn't be tonight.

Was somebody walking at the other end of the hall? Vanessa blinked to focus better and looked again. The hall was empty. She pushed the elevator button again, harder this time. Where was that damned elevator?

She'd never work late again without a buddy. She didn't care how much work needed to be done. This was spooking her out.

She jumped at the sudden swish of the doors opening and her breath caught in her throat. She hurried inside and held the button for the lobby until the doors closed. Resting her shoulder against the elevator wall, she let out a deep breath.

Once in the lobby she told the night guard about the light being out upstairs. The distance from the building to her car was short. She couldn't wait to get home and catch the rest of the Lakers game.

As Vanessa pulled into her drive, she caught a glimpse of something on her front porch. A large package rested against her front door. She pulled into the detached single-car garage and got out. The backyard was darker than usual, so she walked around to the front.

For the first year, she loved her house, but now the thrill was gone. She wanted a two-car garage so she'd have more room for storage. She also wanted more distance between herself and her weed-smoking neighbors. In hindsight, cluster homes were too close for comfort. Her promotion would afford her the opportunity to move from Oak Trace to a larger home, maybe not as large as Betty's, but not another cluster.

She grabbed the package and went inside. She wasn't expecting anything via FedEx. Once inside her office, she flipped on the light and sat down.

In midrip, she stopped and looked at her desk. "What a mess. Did I leave it like this?" She wasn't a neat freak by any stretch of the imagination, but she couldn't remember leaving her folders in such disarray.

She pushed everything aside. "I'll straighten this mess up later." She ripped open the envelope and pulled out the contents. Half expecting something from her mother, she found instead a letter addressed to her, signed *Christopher Harris*. Her hands began to tremble.

Dear Vanessa,

I hope this letter doesn't find you too late.

I've come across something you really need to see. I need you to meet me at China Moon on Wednesday night at eight o'clock.

Here are some papers I want you to look at. We'll discuss them when we meet. Please, don't mention this to anyone at work.

Christopher Harris.

Eric examined the package again. "This is an old envelope. There's no tracking information. Whoever sent this, delivered it personally."

Vanessa sat on the couch, eyeing Detective Daniels as

he leaned against her desk. He'd gotten there so fast, she wondered if he'd been parked around the corner. For the first time she noticed how smooth and flawless his cocoa complexion was. He was a little over six feet tall and solid as a rock. In some old work clothes, he was even more attractive and masculine than in his suit.

She tried to stay focused on the letter. Christopher had asked her to meet him, to discuss something he'd found. However, the letter was the only thing in the envelope.

"I don't understand. If Christopher didn't mail that package before he died, who found it, and why give it to me? Why not show it to the police? What am I supposed to do with it?"

"Do you have any clue what might have been attached to that letter? Was he in any trouble at work?"

She shrugged. "No, not that I know of."

"Why would he ask you to meet him someplace when you worked together every day?" He crossed his arms.

She didn't like the accusing look he gave her. "How would I know?" Vanessa's guard went up. "I don't even know if that letter's from him. It could be somebody's idea of a sick joke." She picked up one of the throw pillows from the couch and squeezed it.

"You said you two worked well together. Exactly what did Christopher do from day to day?"

"He handled the larger accounts. And the collection work I told you about."

"How? By sending out letters?"

"Most of the time. Sometimes he'd have to call the clients and set up payment plans. Or he'd run by to pick up checks from local companies."

"He handled the checks personally?"

"Only a few. And only if he thought they were on the verge of not paying. I told you we had a perfect record in collections. Christopher was good at his job."

"Obviously he was very good." Eric picked the package up from her desk. "If you don't mind, I'm gonna have to take this."

"Sure. Anything to help you find out what's going on. You still think it was suicide?"

Eric tilted his head as if to say he wasn't sure, but he couldn't. "My job is to find out if any criminal act was the cause of his death. Right now, I'm searching for motive of any type."

"You don't think whoever delivered that package had a motive to kill Christopher, do you?" Her voice trembled.

"I don't have a clue. Like you said, we don't even know if the letter's authentic or not."

She tucked one foot under her. "I wish those papers had been attached to that letter. Now I want to know what's going on."

Eric had slipped the letter into a sheet protector. He'd arranged to have it examined. Sitting at his desk reading the letter again, he wondered what it meant. Why did someone leave it at Vanessa's door? And what had they hoped she'd do with it?

"Say, I left a note on your desk pertaining to that guy found down by the Chattahoochee." Eric's partner, Detective Robert Harper, walked past with a cup of coffee in his hand.

Harper was several inches shorter than Eric. His stocky build and crew-cut hairstyle resembled that of a military man.

"Yeah, uh-huh." Eric didn't look up from the letter.

"What you got there?" Harper took a seat at his desk opposite Eric's.

Eric scratched at the back of his ear. "Something that doesn't make sense." He dropped the letter on his desk and leaned back in his seat.

"Let me ask you something."

"Shoot." Harper sipped from his cup.

"If you were about to commit suicide, would you write me a letter asking me to meet you a week later to discuss some work papers?"

Harper shrugged and laughed. "What's this? A trick question? Why would I send the letter if I planned to kill myself?"

"My point exactly." Eric pointed at Harper.

"Something to do with the Harris case?"

"Yeah. A coworker of the victim found this letter on her front porch last night. It's dated a couple of days before the body was found. I'm having it analyzed to verify the signature."

"Did that autopsy come back yet?"

"Yeah, but it didn't determine any other cause of death than suicide. I called Simmons. I like for him to do my autopsies."

"He's busy, you know. That'll take a while."

"I know, but it'll make me feel better."

"You think maybe the family's right?"

Eric picked up his pencil and tapped the eraser against his desk. "If they are, then I need to start digging up a motive for murder."

Four

Vanessa woke up Saturday morning determined to clean up her office and file away some of her folders. She couldn't believe she'd left it in such bad shape in the first place.

She was knee-deep in folders and scraps of papers when the doorbell rang. She looked over at the paperweight clock on her desk. A token from Brightline, for going above and beyond. Who was ringing her bell at ten on a Saturday morning? It couldn't be Betty. They were in Savannah for the weekend. And her mother was in Chicago visiting relatives. She stood, dropped her folders, and went to answer the door. Before she reached the door, the bell rang again.

"Hold your horses." She looked through the peephole. A young white woman stood on the other side looking out toward the street.

"Who is it?" Vanessa asked through the door.

The woman turned around and talked into the peephole.

"Hello, I'm looking for Vanessa Benton."

"What can I help you with?" For all she knew this woman could have left the envelope on her porch. She wasn't about to open her door.

"My name is Gina Harris. I'm Christopher's sister." She paused and cleared her throat before continuing. "I'd like to talk with you for a few minutes if it's okay."

Vanessa opened the door to a tanned white woman with shoulder-length blond hair. So this was Gina. She'd heard Christopher talk about his sister before. She also remembered seeing her at the funeral.

"Hello, I'm Vanessa."

"Hi. May I talk with you a moment?"

Gina's eyes were puffy, and she looked as if she hadn't slept in days. The pleading look on her face caused Vanessa to motion her in. "Come on in."

"Thank you."

Vanessa closed the door behind her. "Have a seat."

Gina walked over to the couch; Vanessa followed. Did she want to know if Christopher had said or done anything to indicate he might take his own life? She couldn't remember how many times she'd answered that question in the last week.

"I hope I'm not disturbing you?" Gina asked, crossing her legs at the ankles.

Vanessa eased into the love seat across from her. "No problem. It's nice to finally meet you. Christopher talked about you often." She had the same prominent nose as Christopher's.

"Same here. He talked about you often, too. That's why I'm here. I need your help." She leaned forward, her eyes pleading with Vanessa.

I knew she wanted something. Instead of asking Gina what she could do for her, Vanessa nodded her head, not sure what to expect.

"You see"—Gina's voice cracked—"my brother is—was—one of the most honest people I've ever known. Over the years he'd saved up plenty of money, so he didn't need to steal anything from Brightline. And he had no reason on this green earth to kill himself."

"I believe you," Vanessa said. She looked down at Gina's lap as she wrung her hands over and over again.

"I even told the police as much. Did you know that he was going on vacation in a few weeks?"

Gina shot a suspicious glance at Vanessa. "No, I didn't. Did he say where he planned on going?"

"Tennessee, I think, somewhere up in the mountains. He was going to rent a cabin or something."

Gina sat back and glanced around the room, nodding as if she were thinking. "I've been reading up on suicides, not that I had to to know my brother didn't kill himself. But from what I read, people about to commit suicide don't make long-range plans." She uncrossed her legs and tapped her feet against the floor.

"I know. I read the same thing."

"He was planning on leaving Brightline. He'd purchased a home in Alabama." She stopped wringing her hands and placed them on her lap.

Vanessa's eyebrows shot up. "I didn't know that." She was learning a lot about her coworker since his death.

Gina leaned forward again, as if she was about to whisper a secret. "I'm sure he told you about the list?" Her eyes widened as they searched Vanessa's face for some sign of recognition.

Vanessa shrugged and shook her head. "List for what?"

Gina sighed. "That's what I hoped you could help me with. He came over last week and started talking about how he had to be careful, something about being targeted on the list." Shifting again on the seat, her voice began to crackle. "I could kick myself for not paying more attention at the time, but I didn't know how important it was. You see, Christopher was always complaining about something. That's just the way he was."

Vanessa gave her a sideways glance and leaned back in her seat. "You think somebody at work had something to do with his death?"

Gina shook her head. "I'm almost certain of it."

Vanessa knew there was more to Christopher's death than suicide. But who at Brightline would want him dead? "Have you talked with the police?"

"Yes, but they aren't interested in what really happened to my brother. He had the gun in his hand, so to them that equals suicide. You have to help me."

"How can I help?" Vanessa gave her a bewildered look.

"You worked there. You must have heard something about that list he was referring to?"

"I'm afraid I haven't."

"But you can find out for me, can't you? I mean, you know a lot of people there, don't you?"

"Of course I do, but—"

"Vanessa, my brother was murdered and I know it involved his work. The only person at Brightline who can help me is you. You worked the same accounts. How could he steal any money without you knowing about it?"

A horrible feeling all but swallowed Vanessa. If Gina came to that conclusion, maybe everyone else would, too. Including whoever killed Christopher. She suddenly felt sick.

"Gina, I know Christopher didn't steal any money. But I'll tell you what—I promise to go through all the accounts we touched. If there's a penny difference, I'll find it. Whatever they've discovered, I'm sure it can be explained."

Gina sighed and leaned back as if a weight was lifted from her shoulders. "Thank you. You don't know how much this means to me."

Or how much it could mean to me, Vanessa thought. "Don't thank me yet. I don't know what I'll find, if I find anything. But I'll try."

"I can't ask for more than that."

* * *

Eric pulled up to Vanessa's house. He flipped down the sun visor and raised the mirror cover. Taking a quick glance in the mirror, he smoothed his hand over his mustache.

When Vanessa opened the front door, she had on workout gear, with an oversize jacket. The jacket covered her chest, but didn't hide all her sexy curves. Eric's heartbeat quickened as he struggled to keep his eyes on her face. He slid his shades down slowly before taking them off. She looked even hotter than she did the last time he saw her.

"Detective Daniels, what a surprise!" She stepped back, resting one hand on her hip.

"I hope it's a pleasant surprise."

She smiled, shaking her head. "Unless you've come to arrest me for something, yes, it is. Come on in."

"Did I come by at a bad time?" he asked, stepping into the foyer area.

"No, I was about to have dinner. I hope you're hungry."

"I could use a bite, yeah."

"I was cooking out back on the grill. It's such a nice evening." She closed the door behind him and motioned for him to follow her. "You don't mind, do you?"

"No, not at all." He followed her through the house. Her jacket stopped right above her rear end, giving him a wonderful view. He talked to the body swaying in front of him. His eyes traveled down the back of her knees to her calves. Those little ankle socks gave him a good view of her sexy smooth calves. Powell was right; he was a leg man.

"So, what brings you by?"

"Two things actually. The letter you received the other night was a phony."

She stopped and looked back over her shoulder. "You're kidding, right?"

"I'm afraid not. Looks like somebody's idea of a sick joke." He cleared his throat. "Unless of course, you have an idea where it came from?"

She looked over him piercingly. "Detective, is that what you came by here for, to accuse me of writing that letter myself?"

He held both hands up. "I never said that. But it is my job to ask."

She continued into the kitchen. Once inside she grabbed a pot holder and a large fork. "Like I said, I found it on my front step."

He shook his head. "I also dropped by Brightline today and spoke with Mr. Steel." Eric held the back door open for her.

"That's nice."

"We discussed the fifty thousand dollars your partner was accused of taking."

She stopped in the doorway and looked up at him. "He's *accused* of taking—remember that." She continued out onto the deck.

"Why don't you talk to me about the checks he handled? Not everything was sent to accounting, was it?"

She raised the grill and motioned for him to pick up a plate from the table. He held the plate out for her.

"No, but whenever he picked up a check, or one was mailed to him, he carried it to accounting. There's nothing wrong with that. Clients get confused. Since they deal with us so much, sometimes they mail the check to us instead of accounting."

"Whom were the checks made out to?"

"Oh, uh, we had them made out to us, of course. How else could we cash them and buy big fine homes and cars?" She gave him a sarcastic smirk. "Brightline, of course. Why would they make a check out to us?"

So, she had a sense of humor. Eric grinned as he leaned back from the smoke heading toward his face. He looked at the meat she pulled off the grill, wondering what the hell it was.

"I wasn't—"

"Yes, you were, Detective. You came by here to ask if I stole money with Christopher . . . Didn't you?" Having taken all the food from the grill, she closed the lid and set her utensils down.

"Did you?" He looked into her eyes for a sign of nervousness. He wasn't totally convinced she was so innocent. Did she know anything she wasn't telling him?

She smiled. "Take your jacket off, Detective. You look hot." She took the plate from him, and set it on the table.

As Eric slid out of his jacket and hung it across the back of a chair, she went inside and brought out a huge salad. "Have a seat. What would you like to drink?" she asked, leaving the door open as she walked back inside.

"Whatever you have, it'll be fine."

She returned with two glasses of water and paper plates. She set his plate and drink in front of him. "Dig in."

Eric watched her fix her plate. She'd totally ignored his question. She fixed her burger then passed him the fork. He took it and picked up one of the patties. "What is this, anyway?"

"Black-bean burgers."

He dropped the patty back on the plate and set his fork down. "You know, I'm not too hungry, after all."

"Suit yourself." She started eating.

"You never answered my question."

"He's innocent. So how could I have helped him?"

"Mr. Steel seems to think otherwise. Apparently, the company's been tracking Christopher's transactions for months. If he's innocent, why do you think someone is trying to pin this on him?"

She stopped chewing and put her burger down. "I

don't have a clue. Christopher's sister, Gina, came by on Saturday to ask me for help, and asked the same thing."

"The family believes he was murdered, too, but so do most suicide victims' families. Suicide is a hard thing for parents to accept. But they can't offer the police any evidence."

Eric sat back and watched Vanessa eat. Enjoying the evening with a beautiful woman didn't feel like hard work. Even if it was only for a moment.

"So that's why she came to me asking for help. I think she expects me to find some of that evidence you're talking about."

"If there's more to this case, I think you'd better leave it to the police. You wouldn't want to get mixed-up in anything, if you aren't already."

The look Vanessa gave him spoke more than words. She stood, kicking her chair back, then picked up her plate. He watched her nostrils flare, as she walked back into the house with her plate.

His moment was over. He stood and picked up his jacket. Holding out one arm, he slung his arm into the jacket, and started into the house at the same time. He came to an abrupt stop as Vanessa walked right out into his chest.

Luckily, she didn't have anything in her hand. Eric reached out and grabbed her by the arms to keep her from falling backward. Doing so pulled her closer to him. Her hands landed in the middle of his chest. He froze with his jacket half-on, half-off.

"Be careful, Detective. I might steal something from you," she alluded with a wicked grin.

Like my heart, he wanted to say aloud. Instead, he let go of her arms as she stepped back. He finished putting on his jacket. "Sorry, I didn't see you coming out. Well, I'd better be leaving."

"Detective—"

"Please, call me Eric."

"Eric, you don't have to worry about me playing detective. I know my job. I just hope you know yours."

He smiled. Her cocky attitude had returned. Time for him to leave. "Ms. Benton, thank you for the time, and the information."

"Call me Vanessa. Everyone does."

He bit his lip to keep from smiling like some schoolboy. She was toying with him, and he loved it. But he needed to stay focused on the case.

"Vanessa, before I go, I need to ask you one last question."

She crossed her arms. "You always do."

"You seem so sure Mr. Harris was killed. Do you have anything to base that on? Anything at all?"

Vanessa reached one hand up to her mouth as she bit her lip. She looked off into the yard as if she saw something in the shrubs. Slowly, she shook her head, then looked up at him. "Nothing but a gut feeling."

She escorted him through the house to the front door. Neither said a word. She opened the front door and Eric stepped outside. "I bet you can't find a reason why he'd commit suicide, either, can you?" she asked.

Eric turned and looked at her, weighing how to answer that question. "I'm looking into it. But no, he doesn't fit the typical suicide."

"Then you have to look for something else, don't you?"

"I need a motive and a suspect. That's why I'm here."

Vanessa walked out back to clean up the grill and bring her things inside. Her back deck was one thing she enjoyed about the house.

She'd enjoyed Detective Daniels visit, too. Although she'd never in a million years admit it to him. Maybe they could work out together sometimes. No, no, she shook her head. "Get that thought out of your head." No matter how good-looking or well built, he was still a cop.

Back inside, she went into her office and sat down to write out some bills. She couldn't get Eric out of her head. Did he really suspect her of stealing, too? Or did he use that as an excuse to come see her? She dipped her index finger into the bowl of water on her desk and ran it across her mortgage bill, then sealed it.

Her brain was working overtime trying to second-guess the detective. In case he suspected her of something, she had better keep her promise to Gina. First thing in the morning, she needed to get into Christopher's files. Hopefully, she'd be able to help him, and save herself.

Vanessa waited around until most of her coworkers were at lunch. She'd walked back to the file room earlier to make sure the door was unlocked. Everyone but Brenda was gone.

"Brenda, you not going to lunch today?" she called out.

Brenda stood and leaned over the petition. "I'm gonna grab a sandwich from the cafeteria. How about you?"

"I'm not hungry."

"I can bring you something back, if you're that busy. Girl, you can't go all day without eating."

Vanessa shrugged as if she didn't care about food at all. "I guess I could eat a sandwich." She reached down and grabbed her purse. This was a good way to get rid of Brenda. "Okay, I'll take a turkey on wheat with mustard."

She waited until Brenda left before walking down the hall. Only a few people were left at their desk. With their heads buried in work, she wasn't worried about being caught.

At the end of the hall was the file room. Nikki, the departmental secretary, was usually the only one who used the file room. All the files were kept locked for some reason. Company policy. Earlier that morning, Vanessa had borrowed the keys to the supply cabinet and unlocked Christopher's file at the same time.

Now she came back to check out his old files. She kept most of her old files at her desk, as she was sure most of her peers did. She carried a few files with her so she could pretend to be filing them away if anyone happened upon her.

She slipped into the room and pulled the door behind her. File cabinets lined the walls all the way around the room. In the center of the room stood two more rows of cabinets. She walked along, running her finger across the file cabinets, until she reached the file labeled Harris. After opening all five drawers and finding two of them empty, she returned to the top file and began flipping through.

"What are you looking for?" A voice came from nowhere.

Five

Vanessa jumped as her heart lodged in her throat. She looked up to see Brenda standing inside the door. She grabbed her chest with one hand, and held on to the file drawer with the other. "Girl, you scared the hell out of me."

Brenda came closer. "I didn't mean to scare you. What you all nervous for? Doing something you shouldn't be doing?" she asked with a grin on her face.

Vanessa didn't even want Brenda to know what she was doing. "No, just putting away some old files. How did you know I was in here?"

"You weren't at your desk, but I knew you couldn't be too far away."

"I forgot to ask what you wanted on your sandwich. I think you always get mustard, but I wasn't sure."

"You came back up here for that?"

Brenda shrugged. "Yes, I know how finicky you are about your food." She stepped closer and looked down at the files Vanessa had laid on the top drawer.

"I thought I said mustard." She looked down at the files with Brenda. "These are just some old accounts I needed to file away." She picked up the files and shoved them into the drawer.

"Bren, do me a favor. On your way out, if you see Nikki, divert her down the hall somewhere. You know, there's too many eyes in this place."

Brenda shook her finger at Vanessa. "I knew you weren't supposed to be in here. Be careful, girl. I'll do what I can." She checked up and down the hall before she slid out, closing the door behind her.

Vanessa hoped Brenda hadn't noticed she was in Christopher's file cabinet and not her own. She sifted through more files, finally stumbling across something she didn't recognize. "ORICA Services." She read the name aloud. She had no memory of setting up this account. She pulled the folder out and laid it on top of the other files. In the back of the file was the information page, which she usually created. She hadn't created this one. She folded the page and quickly inserted it into her jacket pocket.

The file was tucked back and she kept searching. She didn't know what she was looking for, but she kept looking for something that seemed out of the ordinary. Anything that jumped out at her or set off an alarm when she saw it. Taking her time, she was halfway through the files when—

"Who gave you the keys to *that* file cabinet?" came a pretentious voice in the doorway.

Startled, Vanessa jumped and dropped the file on the floor. Nikki stood in the doorway with her hands on her hips. Twenty-four-year-old Nikki Taylor, a single parent of two beautiful little boys, knew her job well. And Vanessa knew Nikki well, and knew she'd jump as high as her boss told her to. Looks like he'd told her to lock Christopher's files and stand guard.

Nikki walked toward Vanessa in her three-inch heels and a suit that looked too expensive for a single parent with two children. "How did you get in there?"

Vanessa recovered the file, closed it, and shoved it back into the cabinet. "It was unlocked," she said innocently. She shoved the other files in the cabinet, as well.

Nikki reached over and slammed the cabinet shut, then

pushed in the lock. "This cabinet is to remain locked at all times." She narrowed her eyes at Vanessa with suspicion.

"Why are you getting all bent out of shape? I had some of his old files I needed to file away."

"Mr. Steel said no one's to go into those files under any circumstance. They're sealed. I thought I locked that cabinet. I could lose my job over this." Her expression changed from suspicion to fear.

Vanessa shrugged. "I won't mention it if you don't. No need for you to get into trouble over this."

Nikki's facial expression softened. She pushed her long blond hair behind her ear and bit the side of her jaw. "Well, I won't let Mr. Steel know you were rummaging through sealed files, if you don't mention the cabinet wasn't locked."

Nice how she turned that around, Vanessa thought. One day she'd be running the company. "It's as good as forgotten," Vanessa said, brushing her hands together.

"Thank you." Nikki looked relieved as she turned to leave the room.

Vanessa followed her. Before Nikki walked out, Vanessa decided to pump her for a little information. "Nikki, I need to ask you something. But you can't mention it to anyone."

Nikki stopped with her hand on the doorknob. She raised one brow, waiting for the question.

"Have you heard anything about a company hit list?"

"A list for what?" she asked, looking surprised.

Vanessa wanted to hit her. Forget about her running the company. Sleeping your way to the top couldn't help this woman.

"That's what I'm trying to find out. Rumor is, there's a list of people the company plans to fire. It might have something to do with the people who've left so far."

Nikki shook her head slowly at first, then faster. "I don't know anything about it."

"Are you sure Mr. Steel didn't bring it up over lunch or dinner sometime?"

The look in Nikki's eyes could have set Vanessa ablaze. Vanessa had always suspected there was more than a boss-employee relationship going on there. Now Nikki confirmed it.

"I'm positive," Nikki said between clenched teeth, and yanked the door wider.

"Then I guess it's just that—a rumor. If you're the hub of this department and you don't know about it, I'm sure it doesn't exist."

"I'm sure it doesn't." She stormed out of the file room and down the hall.

Vanessa walked back to find her supposed lookout, Brenda.

"Betty, I can't believe these old chairs turned out so well. They look brand-new. They're beautiful." Gladys rubbed her hand along the fabric before sitting to test each chair.

"Mama, you act like you've never seen chairs before," Vanessa commented as Gladys moved from one to the other.

"Don't you remember these chairs, darling?" Gladys asked.

"No. Should I?" Vanessa didn't ever remember seeing anything old in Betty's house.

"They used to be in my living room years ago. Remember the gold French Provincial furniture I gave to my mother when I left New York? You probably don't remember; you were so young. After Grandmama died, Betty and Harold went to get them and stored them in the garage. I'm just so proud of the way she restored them. These were a wedding present from your grandfather when I got married."

"They're that old?"

Gladys cut her a sharp look.

Betty walked into the room. "They're antiques, but I wouldn't expect you to know anything about that. If it's old, you throw it out. No matter what condition it's in."

Betty was a Mini-Me version of Gladys. The women were so much alike, Vanessa sometimes wondered if she wasn't adopted. Her mother kept telling her she was just like her father, but without him around, she couldn't be sure.

"Let's just say I'm not into antiques and leave it at that. I'm surprised you didn't just run out and charge some new chairs instead of fixing up those old ones."

Vanessa knew Harold Williams took good care of his family. He'd purchased a three-hundred-thousand-dollar home that Betty loved decorating. Her life revolved around her son, and the Home and Garden Channel.

A miniature version of Harold came running into the room. He ran over to Vanessa and stood between her legs looking up at her.

"There's my little man." She reached down and pulled her nephew, Reggie, up onto her lap. "You ready to party tonight?"

He smiled and pointed at her face, trying to reach her nose. *Mama, stop,* and a few more hard-to-understand words were the extent of his vocabulary when he didn't feel like talking. She took his smile as a yes.

"There will be no partying in this house tonight." Betty walked over and picked up her son. "Reggie, are you going to be good for Aunt Vanessa tonight?" She kissed him several times on the cheek.

"He's always good. Like I said, you've got the perfect house, perfect husband, and a perfect son."

Betty gave him back. "I know." She placed her hands

on her hips and wiggled as she walked away, looking big and sassy.

Betty and Gladys left for an evening at one of Betty's volunteer galas. After an hour of playing with her nephew, Vanessa popped in one of his Barney videos. She sang along with him for a while, then took a seat on the couch. What she wouldn't give for a little boy, or girl for that matter. As long as a good husband came along with it, like Harold.

While Reggie stared transfixed at the purple dinosaur, Vanessa went into the kitchen and flipped open the folders she'd brought with her. The information sheet she'd pulled out on ORICA Services was compared against transactions Christopher had made in the last six months. She couldn't find the company on the regional report that circulated to the executives. However, she'd pulled a second record of transactions on a lower level, and there it was. Something funny was going on. Why hadn't she heard of this company before? The process was she'd set up the accounts, Christopher drew up the contracts, then they processed fee payments together.

She walked over to the couch and pulled her cell phone from her purse. She dialed the contact phone number on the information sheet, which was long-distance.

"I'm sorry, the number you've reached is no long—"

She hung up, and went back into the kitchen and through the folders with a fine-tooth comb. There had to be something here she was missing. If the company didn't exist, then how was a payment approved?

Finally she noticed something else that didn't make sense. ORICA Services had the exact same amount of transactions and products sold as another company at the same time, which was unusual. Normally, payments never matched up like that.

She wondered if Gina could be right. Did Christopher

stumble upon something that someone didn't want him to? Could the answer be hidden within his files?

She hadn't heard a peep out of Reggie for a while. When she peeked into the den, he was fast asleep in the middle of the floor, on the plush carpet, and Barney was singing away on the television screen.

She found Eric's business card and dialed his home number.

"Hello." He answered his voice a little huskier than usual.

His deep sexy voice sent a shiver through her. Had she woken him? She wanted to know what he looked like when he slept. "This is Vanessa Benton. You weren't asleep, were you?"

"No. Is something wrong?" he asked, sounding more alert now.

"Not actually, but you did say to call if I found out anything."

"I did. You haven't received any more packages, have you?"

"No, but I've found something I think might be worth looking into."

"I'm listening."

"I found these files that don't make sense. It's a little hard to explain over the phone. You kind of need to see what I'm looking at."

"Want me to come over?"

He sounded too eager. "No, I'm not at home right now anyway. I could drop them off tomorrow at the police station, I guess. Or, even better—you could meet me somewhere tomorrow."

"How about lunch tomorrow downtown somewhere? I know how the station bothers you."

"It's not just the station that bothers me." She wanted to elaborate since he seemed like such a nice guy, but she decided to be cautious. "Okay, we can meet at—"

"If you don't mind me asking, what bothered you so much when you came down for the interview? I hope it wasn't me."

"No, it wasn't you."

"I'm glad to hear that. So why did you give me such a hard time?"

"I wasn't aware I did. For once I'd like to see the police do their job. I'd hate to see Christopher's case close knowing there's a murderer out there."

"So that's it. You have no faith in the police? I'm not sure what caused that, but I can assure you that if your friend didn't commit suicide, I'll find out."

"That's all anybody wants, is for you to do your job. Cops are always—"

"Hold on there. Before you start with the stereotyping, you need to give me a chance. I think we got off on the wrong foot. So we'll meet tomorrow for lunch and start over. Is that too much to ask for?"

Thank goodness he couldn't see her through the phone. She cradled the phone between her ear and shoulder, while tracing small circles on her folder, smiling.

"I suppose it's not," she said coyly.

"Good."

Silence hung between them. She searched for something to say that wasn't negative and didn't sound like she was picking on him.

"Do I get a hint as to what you've found?" he asked.

"I think I'd better wait until tomorrow." She thought of something she'd wanted to ask him but wasn't sure how. Now, not looking him in the eye, she had the courage to ask.

"Can I ask you something that I hope isn't too tacky?"

"Sure. What?"

"Did you see Christopher? His body I mean?"

He took a deep breath. "No, I wasn't on the scene, if that's what you mean. I was assigned the case three days after his death. The same day I interviewed you. Is there something you want to know that I might be able to answer for you?"

"I just wondered if he got shot on the side of the head or what? I shouldn't be asking that, I'm sorry."

"Don't be. People ask all the time. Actually, it was a gunshot to the temple. How did you guess?"

Vanessa shrugged and detected a note of suspicion in his voice. "I don't know. It was the first thing I thought when you said it was suicide. If you shoot yourself, it's usually in the temple, isn't it?"

"Not necessarily. But I know you don't want all the details of how to shoot yourself in the head."

"Spare me please. That's such a chicken-hearted way to die. And no matter what, I can't see Christopher doing that. Who was he out wi-with?" She jumped after feeling something touch her side.

"You okay?"

She looked down at Reggie rubbing his eyes and poking her in the side with his finger.

"Reggie, you scared me to death." She reached down and rubbed her hand over his little head.

"Reggie wouldn't happen to be your boyfriend, would he?" Eric asked.

"No." She laughed. "He's my nephew. I'm baby-sitting right now. And it's past his bedtime," she commented, looking down at Reggie. "Time to tuck you in bed."

"Lucky fellow," Eric commented.

Vanessa pretended not to hear that. She could picture him standing with his shirt off. His rock-hard chest was the perfect place to lay her head. The pants would have to go next. His long legs and firm thighs wrapped around her is how she wanted to tuck him in.

What was she doing! "Eric, I'd better go. I'll call you tomorrow about lunch."

"Okay, if I'm not at my desk, page me. I won't be too far away."

"Thank you."

Vanessa hung up, blushing over their conversation. She'd flirted with him, and he'd flirted with her. Was she losing her mind? She had no business flirting with a cop. *Never date another cop.* After she turned the folders over to him tomorrow she'd make sure not to contact him again.

Eric walked back out to the garage thinking about Vanessa every step of the way. Her sexy long legs, those luscious poutie lips, her . . .

"Hey, where's my beer?"

Eric looked up at Harper sitting on a yard chair in his garage. He had the chair tilted back, pushing off with his toes. Damn. He snapped his fingers. He forgot the beer. He was supposed to grab one after he answered the phone.

"I knew I forgot something. Be right back." He went back into the house and grabbed a cold beer from the refrigerator. Look what she'd done to him already. A distraction, that's what she was. And the last thing he needed if he was going to solve this case.

He returned to the garage and handed Harper the beer. He walked over to his workbench and picked up his bottle of beer.

"Man, she's coming along pretty good."

Eric almost choked on his beer. He coughed several times and set the bottle down beside him. Was he talking about Vanessa?

"What?"

"The car. You're making some progress. You okay?" He let his chair down.

"Yeah." Eric coughed again to clear his throat. For a

minute there he thought Harper knew Vanessa was on his mind. Instead, he was referring to the 1966 Lincoln Continental he had been restoring.

"What I want to know is when do you get the time to work on her?"

Eric took another swig of beer. "Between cases, or when I'm working a real tough case." He grabbed a rag and walked over to rub off the car. "Yeah, this is how I work out things in my head. Man, sometimes I come out here and work on this old thing for hours. If I had the money I'd be finished by now."

Harper got up and walked over to sit in the front seat. "Yeah, man, I wish my old lady would let me do something like this."

"Tell her you need it to work out your cases. It's a work write-off." Harper joined him in a hearty laugh.

"I don't think that would fly with children in school."

"No, probably not."

"So, what have you worked out on the Harris case so far? Rubbed out some car leather and figured the whole case out, have ya?"

Eric laughed. "Not quite. This one's going to take a little work."

"Any suspects yet? Or, do you think Archer was correct and it's a suicide?"

"You know as well as I do that Archer was living in the bottom of a gin bottle when he turned in his report. I'm looking for a suspect right now."

"I read the report. Looks like the bullet entered on the left side, but the guy was right-handed." Harper took a swig of beer.

"Yeah, but that's not enough to go on. There's no evidence of trauma or a struggle. He was slumped over the steering wheel like a suicide victim." He threw his rag at his toolbox and finished off his beer.

"Still waiting on that autopsy?"

"Yeah. The first one said suicide, but after all the interviews I went through it's tough to believe. The guy wasn't depressed, had no financial problems, he wasn't a drug user, alcohol abuser, or anything. Just your everyday working stiff." He picked up another rag, poured some oil on it, and walked over to open the passenger door.

Harper leaned the driver seat back and looked up at the ceiling of the car. "Get anything else out of his coworker?"

Eric stopped in motion and looked at Harper. "Ms. Benton?"

"Yeah, the one with the sexy legs who called you over the other night."

He bit his bottom lip to hold back a grin. "Actually, that was her who called a few minutes ago. She's found something she wants me to look at. I'm meeting her for lunch tomorrow." He continued rubbing the car door.

"So what's up?" Harper asked with a bit of suspicion in his voice.

"What you mean?" Eric kept wiping, putting more elbow into it this time.

"Come on, this is me you're talking to. Remember? Your partner."

Eric stopped and looked over at him. "She's part of the case, that's all."

"Yeah . . . so was Janet." His right brow shot up.

They exchanged long stares. Eric couldn't believe Harper had gone there. Harper knew her death had taken an emotional toll on Eric. He met her in the same way he met Vanessa—while working a case. He hadn't meant to start a relationship with her, or put her life in danger by falling in love with her.

"Look, man, I'm just saying be careful. If this guy was murdered and it's connected to his job in some way, how do you know she's not involved?"

"She's not," Eric shot back at him, still staring.

Harper set his beer bottle between his legs and held up both hands. "Okay, okay, just watch your back." He grabbed the empty bottle and got out of the car.

Eric inhaled, then let out a deep heavy breath. *What the hell was he getting into?*

Six

"Process this last transaction, then I want you to close the account and file everything away."

"Are you sure it's safe? I mean with everything that's going on."

"Let me worry about that. Just process everything like before." He threw a piece of paper across the table.

"This is crazy. It's too much. You're going to get us arrested."

"You need to stop thinking small. Didn't I take care of you last time?"

"I guess."

"We're about to become very wealthy, and by the time they discover anything, we'll be miles away. Make this one last transaction and we're out of here."

"I don't think this is such a good idea."

"I don't remember asking what you thought. Besides, you're just being paranoid. Relax, everything will work out. Have I ever let you down?"

"Not yet."

"I'll pretend I didn't hear that. You left Boone and Company very comfortable. Nothing's changed."

"Yeah, man, but I still don't like it. The cops have been here twice already. What if somebody starts snooping around?"

"If they do, I'll take care of it."

"Yeah, well, whose name goes on this one?"
"The same as last time. Vanessa Benton."

Vanessa met Eric at Copeland's for seafood. She hoped she was doing the right thing by turning over to the police what may be her only clue. She slid two folders across the table to Eric. He leafed through the pages inside.

"I've put Post-its on the sections I think you should look at."

He ran his finger down the page. He stopped and scratched behind his ear as he shrugged. "Exactly what am I looking at?"

"Payments made." She scooted her chair around the circular table, closer to him, leaned over, then ran her finger down the column she wanted him to see.

"See here, the dates and amounts are identical. Not once in the two years I've been on the job have I seen two customers sell the exact same products at the same time, and have them contracted for the same percentages."

When she looked up, she caught Eric gazing up her arm until he reached her face. She didn't see cold cop eyes. Instead, his eyes were those of a hungry man—and not for seafood. For a minute, she thought he would reach out and kiss her. Remembering their conversation last night, she didn't jerk away like she normally would have. Instead, she sat up with ease, then broke her gaze from him.

"So that proves . . . ?" he asked.

"Huh?" *What were they talking about?*

"The payments not matching. What does that prove?"

The waiter arrived with their orders. After setting the food down, he cleared out of their way.

"Something not right. The same percentages paid

aren't strange, but the same transactions for the same amounts? There's something like a million-to-one chance of that happening, I bet."

He closed the folder and picked up his napkin.

"I don't have all the answers. That's your job. What do you want? Me to find the clues and solve the crime, too?" She threw up her arms before moving her chair back to its original spot.

Eric leaned back laughing.

Now she wasn't so sure she'd done the right thing. She placed her napkin in her lap and said a quick prayer.

"It's not funny. My job might be on the line."

His laughter died down. "I thought this was about Christopher."

"It is, but if those accounts have Christopher's name on them, mine has to be there somewhere, too. We handled everything together. And if they're linked to the theft he's accused of, maybe you can prove he didn't do it."

"Which would also prove your innocence?"

"I haven't been accused of anything, but yes, if it comes to that."

Eric didn't say anything for a few minutes while they ate. Vanessa had such a serious look on her face he knew she was scared of something.

"You know, your friend's suicide does raise some questions."

"Like what?" she asked eagerly.

"I can't go into detail, but after conducting all the interviews, we can't find any problems that would cause him to commit suicide. Unfortunately, I don't see any motive for murder, either. I've ordered another autopsy, so I'll know more once it comes back."

"How long does that take?"

He shrugged. "They're pretty backlogged right now. I'm not sure."

"Eric, charging him with theft a day or two before he dies is just too convenient. It has something to do with those funny accounts, I'm telling you."

"I'll have them looked at."

"Can't the police pull company records? You should be able to dig down into what's really going on."

He shook his head. "Without probable cause I can't just walk into Brightline and ask to go through their records."

"Why not? You're the police."

"Vanessa, as soon as I come up with something substantial, I'll pick that place apart."

"What I gave you wasn't enough?"

He looked down at the file. "I'll let you know after I've looked through it."

"So, we're back at square one. No evidence, no nothing, just a suicide." She sat back pouting.

"Vanessa, I need to see you in my office a minute please." Jane stood looking over the cubical at Vanessa.

"Sure." Vanessa dropped everything and followed her boss. Brenda gave her a "what's up?" look as she walked away. Vanessa hunched her shoulders while mouthing "I don't know." She hoped this was about her promotion.

Jane closed the door after Vanessa walked in. "Have a seat."

Jane's tone wasn't a pleasant one. What had Vanessa done to be summoned? Maybe they had found a way to pin something on her, too. She tried to relax and not be so paranoid.

"Vanessa, how's your workload?"

She thought carefully before answering. It sounded like a new *opportunity* was headed her way. "It's manageable. I've got payments ready to be made. Who's going to pick up Christopher's half of the job?"

"That's what I wanted to talk with you about. Right now, we can't afford to backfill his position. I've looked at the workload and everybody seems to be pretty overloaded right now. That could be a good thing for you."

Here comes opportunity, Vanessa thought. "In what way?"

"Christopher was a few levels higher than you. If you pick up his part of the job, and process everything to completion, you could be working toward a promotion."

"Could be?"

"You would be. I can't give you the promotion right away because of the state of the business, but we can look at it down the road."

Did she miss something, or was her boss losing her mind? "What about the promotion to contracts I'd applied for? I was hoping that would come through."

"There's a freeze on those jobs right now, but as soon as things open up down the road, you'll be the first one considered."

"How far down the road are we talking? And can I get that in writing?"

Jane laughed and shook her head. "I'll see what I can do. You're up for a review in a few weeks. We can put this in your development plan and set the stage for a level upgrade if nothing else."

"Does this mean that I'll have access to all of Christopher's files? Old and new?"

Jane lowered her eyes before sifting through papers on her desk. "Not quite. I have a list here of the accounts you will be picking up. You won't be given full access to everything, but enough for you to process payments." She looked up at Vanessa, smiling nervously. "Because of the charges, you understand." She handed over a small stack of files.

Vanessa fingered through them. She didn't see the new

accounts she'd discovered. "How about access to his soft copy files?"

"No, you don't need those."

This was ridiculous. How did they expect her to process the payments without going into accounts he'd set up in *his* computer? "How can I process the payments if the accounts were set up in Christopher's system?"

Jane shrugged. "Can't you create an account in your system?"

That was the problem with having a boss who didn't know the job. Anyone on the floor knew that was impossible without creating an accounting nightmare. "Jane, I can, but that—"

"Then do it. They're not going to give us access to Christopher's system. But we have to get these accounts closed. And if you can close those out within the week, I'd appreciate it. Customers have started to escalate on us."

Vanessa wanted to jump across the desk and slap her. Jane had no idea how much work she was asking of her. Not to mention that Vanessa had new accounts coming in daily. Before she could even think of anything else, Jane stood.

"If you need help, just let me know. I know it's an awful lot of work, and I promise to see that you're compensated for it. I've got faith in you, Vanessa, and I know you can handle it. Once you get the accounts set up, send me a spreadsheet so I'll know what you're working on."

Vanessa walked out of there gritting her teeth. She wasn't about to create all these accounts all over again. Somehow she had to find a way to get into Christopher's system. She'd create a spreadsheet for Jane, but she wasn't reinventing the wheel. Besides, she told herself, this might be her way of finding more evidence once she got into his system.

* * *

"Okay, folks, now that we've taken care of last week's numbers, we've got some serious business to talk about. As you know, a former employee, Christopher Harris, was confronted a day before his untimely death about stealing fifty thousand dollars from us." Vince Steel, the director of processing for Brightline, Inc. looked around the table at his management staff. All heads were bowed as they acknowledged the death.

"I've talked to the police, and I want to make sure what we have on Mr. Harris was solid." He turned to Christopher's manager. "Mitch, I want to go over all the evidence you generated again. Have it on my desk by close of business."

"Yes, sir. It'll be on your desk before you leave today."

"Good. Jane, are you taking care of accounting?"

"Yes, sir. They're conducting an internal audit. If there's more stealing going on, we'll find it."

"Great. Looks like we've got everything taken care of."

"Vince, there is something else I'd like to point out." Mitch cleared his throat to get everyone's attention.

"And that is?" Vince asked.

"His partner. Didn't Christopher work with Vanessa Benton?"

Jane spoke up. "Yes, he did. But what does she have to do with anything?"

"I just don't want us to overlook an obvious fact."

"Which is?" Jane asked defensively.

"She worked on those accounts, I'm sure. How do we know for certain she didn't have anything to do with this whole mess? Is anyone looking into that?"

"I don't think we need to. She's already been questioned by the police, and I can't believe she'd do anything like that."

"That's what you said about Christopher." Mitch looked around the room as if he wanted someone who agreed with him.

"You have a valid point. Mitch, I want you to check her files. If there's a penny missing, I want to know about it," Vince demanded.

"Sure thing, boss." Mitch smiled at Jane. She didn't smile back.

"Hey, girl, what's up?" Brenda hovered over Vanessa's desk the minute she returned from lunch.

"Work. I'm up to my neck in it."

"New accounts?"

"No, Jane gave me some of Christopher's accounts to close out. I have to do his job, and mine."

"I guess that means you're not hanging out tonight?"

"Afraid not."

"You're missing another ball game. Since Christopher's death I haven't been able to get you out for any fun."

"I'll catch the next game."

"What's she got you working on now?"

"I don't know. I haven't even looked at the accounts yet."

Brenda walked around to her desk and leafed through the folders sitting on the corner of Vanessa's desk. "Let's see what we've got here."

"And to add insult to injury, she won't even give me access to his system. I have to create the accounts all over again, and have it done before the week is out."

"Don't worry. I'll help you."

"Thanks, Bren. This time I might take you up on that."

"I insist on helping. As a matter of fact, I think I'll miss the game tonight and get started right now."

"You don't have to do that."

"No problem. Let me make a quick phone call and we can get started."

Brenda could be pretty nosey sometimes, but Vanessa was thankful for her help this time. She always came through in a pinch. She might even be able to help her get into Christopher's system.

The next day at lunch, Vanessa heard something she wasn't prepared for.

"So, what's this about some secret list going around the company?" asked Felicia, one of Vanessa's coworkers.

"What?" Vanessa asked, startled.

"Yeah, girl, I heard there's some list going around with all the people the company plans to fire. Didn't you hear about it?"

Was that the list Gina told her about? "No, I haven't heard a thing. Tell me about it."

"Well, Bonnie told me she thinks Mr. Steel keeps the list locked in his desk. I'm not sure who's on it."

"When did she tell you this?"

"Last week. I'm surprised you haven't heard by now. Everybody's trying to find out if they're on the list. I'm going to update my résumé just in case. You never know in today's market what's going to come next."

That sounded like the list Vanessa asked Nikki about. Had she leaked it out on the floor, or was the rumor already there? If there was such a list, she hoped she could find it first.

When she got back to her desk she had an urgent E-mail announcing a mandatory emergency meeting at two P.M.

"Hey, Bren," she called over her cube. "What's this meeting about?"

Brenda popped up. "I don't know."

"Why don't you go ask Nikki?"

"No way. She doesn't like me any more than she likes you."

"Come on. I see you guys talking. I know you're big buddies," she said with a slight chuckle.

Brenda shook her head. "I was probably begging for some paper clips. It's a crime the way that woman hoards all the supplies. You have to fill out a requisition for a pencil around here. The other day she asked me to justify why I needed a ruler."

"You're kidding. What did you tell her?"

"I said, 'So I can measure how far your nose is up Mr. Steel's butt.' "

They broke out laughing.

Vanessa looked at the clock on her computer. "Well, it's two o'clock, let's go."

"Maybe it's that detective, coming back to talk to everyone," Brenda said as she elbowed Vanessa.

Vanessa glanced over at her, wondering what she meant by that. Did she know Eric had been over to her house on several occasions?

When they walked into the conference room, it was standing room only. The entire department was there. Mitch Waiters stood at the head of the room and cut his eyes at them as they walked in.

Brenda found a spot against the wall and Vanessa squeezed in beside her.

"Now that everyone's here, I'd like to get started." With his hands behind his back, he paced across the front of the room.

"For starters, I want to dispel a rumor I heard. Some of you seem to think there's some list floating around here with the names of employees the company plans to fire." He stopped pacing and looked up at the crowd.

Vanessa thought he was looking right at her.

"Before this nonsense goes any farther, let me assure you it doesn't exist. I don't know how this mess got started, but I don't want to hear about it again." He picked up a stack of papers in front of him. "Any questions about that?"

Several people looked as if they wanted to raise their hand, but didn't. Vanessa started to do it out of spite, but she doubted she'd get any backup if she needed it.

"Moving along, I want to give everyone a quick update on how we're doing this month." He took one sheet and put the rest down. He spent the next twenty minutes covering company progress.

After they returned to their desks, Vanessa wanted to say something to Brenda about Nikki, but she wasn't sure how well acquainted they were.

"I can't believe they called us down there basically to dispel some stupid rumor. Isn't that ridiculous?" Brenda asked.

"I don't know." Vanessa shrugged. "Some people were probably worried about their jobs."

"Well, they should have spoken up. Do you believe management would be dumb enough to create such a list?"

"If they did, they'd never let us know about it. Besides, I didn't hear that anyone had seen the list. Did you?"

Brenda shook her head. "No, probably because it doesn't exist."

Vanessa shrugged. "Maybe no—maybe so."

[illegible]

[illegible] good any farther. If that sounds [illegible] I don't know [illegible] this [illegible] about it much. The [illegible] of him. Any que- [illegible]

[illegible] if they [illegible] than [illegible] but [illegible] exactly.

[illegible]

After they [illegible]

[illegible]

I [illegible] a day.

[illegible] they [illegible] would be done [illegible] such as [illegible]

Kay [illegible] about [illegible] did anyone [illegible] about [illegible] probably [illegible]

[illegible]

Seven

Jarred from a deep sleep by the shrill of the phone, Vanessa groped for the receiver. Who was calling her at two o'clock in the morning?

"Hello," she croaked.

"Vanessa, were you asleep?" Betty's quivering voice came through the phone.

"Of course I was asleep. What's up?" Butterflies fluttered in her stomach. She hated early-morning calls. They usually weren't good news.

Betty sniffled a few times before attempting to clear her throat. "It's two in the morning and Harold isn't home yet."

Vanessa sat up. "Maybe he's out clubbing?"

"Harold doesn't go *clubbing*. He said he had to work late, but it's beyond late."

"Did you call his office, or his cell phone?"

"I've called the office, his cell, his buddies. Nobody's seen him."

"Betty, he's probably hanging out with some guys." Vanessa tried to adjust her eyes in the dark room.

"If I tell you something, you have to promise not to mention it to Mama."

"Of course. What is it?"

"This isn't the first time he's stayed out late. He's been doing it on and off for a few months now."

"You're kidding." Harold didn't drink or smoke, as

far as Vanessa knew. "Where do you think he is?" she asked, stunned.

"I don't know. Every time I ask him, he says he's working late. But, Vanessa, my instincts tell me something is wrong."

Hello! Wake up, big sis.

"You think he's playing around?" She couldn't even believe she was asking her sister that.

"Yes, I think he's been with somebody."

"Harold! Betty, no way. He's too straitlaced of a guy. I can't see him doing anything wrong."

"Well, something's going on. He waits until I'm in the bed before he sneaks in. But tonight I've got a surprise for him. I'm not going to bed. We're going to talk this out tonight!"

After she hung up, Vanessa lay there thinking about life. She thought Betty had everything she herself had ever wanted in life. But things weren't always greener on the other side.

Vanessa drove down Mt. Paran Road, following the directions Gina Harris had given her. The house wasn't hard to find.

She lived in a beautiful three-story, salmon-colored, Spanish-style house with a two-car garage. Nice, Vanessa thought. Very nice, for a single woman with no children.

Gina opened the door on the first ring. "Hello, Vanessa. Come in, and thank you for stopping by."

"Hi," Vanessa said as she walked in, looking around the foyer. This woman wasn't hurting for a thing.

"Let's go into the great room. I have someone I want you to meet."

Today Gina looked as if she'd stepped out of a Ralph Lauren catalog. Her attire fit her and her house, Vanessa thought.

"Gina, I'm afraid I haven't found out much yet. But I did—"

Gina stopped and reached back to touch Vanessa's shoulder. "Don't worry about it. Just come meet my guest."

Classical music filled the great room. A tall blond man stood next to the CD player holding the remote as he switched to another track.

"Sean." When he didn't respond, Gina motioned for Vanessa to follow her. She walked over and tapped him on the shoulder.

He spun around, seeing the ladies, then lowered the volume on the stereo. "I'm sorry. This is such a marvelous piece." He closed his eyes and moved his head to the music. "Don't you just love it?"

"Sure, but not right now." Gina reached over and turned the volume all the way down.

Sean opened his eyes and looked down at the remote.

"Sean, I have someone I want you to meet."

He set the remote on the stereo. "You must be Vanessa Benton," he said, extending his hand. He had to look up to make eye contact. She stood a few inches taller than the both of them.

Vanessa shook his hand and smiled. He was one of the most attractive white men she'd ever had the pleasure of meeting. His baby-blue eyes only added to his appeal. She looked from him over to Gina. Who was this guy, and how did he know her?

"I'm Sean."

He said his name as if she should know who he was. She'd never seen him before.

"Didn't Christopher ever mention Sean?" Gina asked.

Vanessa shook her head and turned down her lips. "I'm afraid not. Or, if he did, I don't recall." She gave Sean an apologetic smile. Was he Christopher's brother?

He didn't look anything like him. He was smaller and thinner than Christopher.

"I'm not surprised, he was such a private person. I don't see how he did it." Sean walked over to the couch and sat down.

Gina motioned for Vanessa to have a seat, as well. She chose an overstuffed chair across from the couch.

"Everybody in my life knew about Chris. It didn't bother me."

Confused, Vanessa looked from Sean to Gina. "Am I missing something here? What do you mean everybody knew about him?"

"Chris was my life partner. In other words, we were lovers."

Her eyes widened instantly. Thrown for a loop, she tried not to look too shocked. She had no idea Christopher was gay. She didn't know quite how to respond, or if she should respond, for that matter.

"Vanessa, I think there was a lot about my brother you didn't know. Now you know why he was an extremely private person. He wasn't openly gay."

"You're right, he was private, because I knew nothing about his life outside of work. But I never asked, either. We didn't have that type of relationship."

"Vanessa, I know I asked for your help. Then I talked to Sean the other day, and I think he can help, too."

"I haven't found out much. Only some strange accounts that I think might lead to something, I'm not sure."

Leaning forward in his seat, Sean spoke up. "Then I think I can help. Sometimes Chris brought work home for the weekend. He showed me some papers I think you might want to look at. He was on to something. I just don't know what."

"Why don't you show them to Detective Daniels?" Vanessa couldn't figure out why they were telling her.

"Vanessa, I'd feel more comfortable if you would look at them first. You see, my father's very involved in our church, and very much against the gay lifestyle. Christopher kept it from him all these years. And I don't think he could take it if he found out now."

Vanessa turned to Sean. "So, you haven't spoken to the police at all?"

He looked at Gina, who had her head down. "No, I haven't. Chris and I have a house in Alabama where he kept a lot of things. I've been staying there."

Vanessa didn't remember seeing him at the funeral, either. But he could have been there, since she wasn't aware he existed. She looked from Gina to Sean. This didn't sound right. What were they trying to get her in the middle of?

"The files in Alabama are from Brightline. It's stuff that you and Chris worked on together, I'm sure. Don't you want to take a look at it?" Gina offered.

Gina knew how to get her interested. Vanessa realized that if she didn't look at the files, they might show them to someone else. "Where in Alabama?"

"Luverne. It's just a little over three hours, not far from here at all. You can drive up and back in a day if you want." Sean spoke up and leaned over in his seat.

No one was offering to go with her.

Sean pulled a key from his pocket. "Here's the key." He walked over to Vanessa and held out the key. "I'm going to be out of town for a little while. You can just give it to Gina when you're through with it."

She stared at the key dangling from his hand. "You want me to drive to Alabama and look through some files and try to find what? Why couldn't you just bring them here?"

"I don't know what's what. I figured if you looked through them, you might find something of value. You might even be able to figure out what was so important it was worth his life."

She took the key. What on earth could she possibly do for these people that the police couldn't? "Okay, but I still think you need to involve the police. I'm no detective."

Gina stood and walked over to the sideboard, which held a tray of small sandwiches and two glasses of wine.

"Vanessa, would you like something to eat?"

"No, thanks, I'm fine." She opened her purse and dropped the key inside. "How do I get to this place in Alabama?"

"I'll write down everything you need to know. Be right back." Sean left the room.

Gina took her sandwich and wine, and returned to the couch. "Vanessa, thank you so much for helping us. My mother passed away a few years ago. She knew about Sean, and accepted it. However, my father is seventy-six years old, and I don't think he could take it. Christopher meant the world to him. The death has already crippled him."

"I'm sorry to hear that. You seem to handle it pretty well."

"Christopher and I were best friends. I guess you could say I'm the only one he felt comfortable talking to, in the family that is. I'm close to Sean, as I am with all of Christopher's friends.

"If you do find something in Alabama that will help, please do let the police know. I'd prefer it came from you if you don't mind."

"Sure." Vanessa wasn't too sure if it was okay or not, but she agreed. She wanted to see where this was going.

Sean returned with a piece of paper he handed to Vanessa. "Everything you need to know is here; directions from Atlanta to my doorstop. Also, my phone number. Please call me if you need to."

"I'll check it out this weekend." Vanessa said as she folded the paper and put it in her purse.

Eric read over the second autopsy. The first copy, from a local hospital pathologist may have said suicide, but this guy, forensic pathologist Syd Otto, knew his stuff. This time, foul play was detected.

"I see you got the autopsy," Harper commented.

"Yeah, and it looks like we've got something here."

"Really?" He took a seat in the chair next to Eric's desk. "What you got?" Harper asked, stretching his neck toward the file.

Eric opened the file. "There was a small trace of gun powder residue on the web of the victim's hand. Which doesn't mean he wasn't forced to pull the trigger. There's also an abrasion above the victim's left eye. I don't think he hit himself in the head, then shot himself."

"Could have. Anything's possible."

"What's possible is that we've got ourselves a homicide. I think I need to talk with the pathologist on this one."

"The chief asked me to help you out with the case, and he wanted to know how close you were to closing."

"This should be enough to talk him into allowing us to keep the case open for a little while longer. Now we need a suspect." He stood and pat Harper on the shoulder. "Welcome aboard. You all finished with the Chattahoochee case?"

"Let's just say it's going slow. I've got some free time."

"Good. Can you round up all the ballistics information for me? I've got to prepare my report for the chief."

"I'll get right on it."

"Thanks. I'm going to catch up with Syd." Eric left

for the pathologist's office. He wanted to know what else Syd had seen but maybe hadn't put on the report.

After a long week, quitting time came. Eric picked up the autopsy report and threw it in his drawer. Time for a little R and R. He'd been so busy with the Harris case he hadn't seen Vanessa all week. But now he had an excuse to visit. He threw some trash in the can and turned to walk away when his phone rang.

He looked at his watch. Answering that call could lead to overtime and ruin his weekend. But then again, it might be Vanessa. He picked up the receiver.

"Detective Daniels."

"Hello, Detective. Are you the one handling Christopher Harris's suicide?"

Eric kicked back his chair. *Have a seat, old boy.* "Yes I am." He searched his desk for a pen.

"Then you're the one I want to talk to."

"Who's this?"

"I'd rather not say. But I think I've got some information for you."

Eric tapped his eraser against the desk. "Yeah, what you got?" A man's voice sounded as if he were holding something over the mouthpiece.

"He didn't kill himself."

"Yeah, how do you know that?" Eric asked, sounding restless. He didn't feel like playing on the phone this evening.

"Because I know who killed him."

Eric sat up straight in his seat. He began scribbling everything down on his pad. Maybe this wasn't a hoax, after all. "Care to share that information?" He tried to see if he recognized the man's voice, but he didn't.

"I can't. But ask his partner." He hung up.

"Damn." Eric slammed the phone down, swore, and

kicked his garbage can, turning it over. He caught the attention of several other detectives who stared at him as he flipped through his book for Vanessa's number.

He looked back over his notes. What did the caller mean by—"ask his partner"? What was Vanessa's connection?

"Hello."

"Vanessa, this is Eric."

"Detective, what a coincidence. I was about to call you. I've got something interesting for you."

"Yeah, well, I must be on everybody's list tonight. What ya got?" *Ask his partner.* Maybe she did know more than she was telling.

"I've got a key to a house in Alabama that I think you might be interested in."

"Sorry, but I'm not in the market for a house right now."

"And I'm not a real-estate agent. It's Christopher's house. I found out the other day that he was working on something and all the papers are there. You might find something to help with the case. I'm going to check it out, but I'm not too gung ho about driving to Alabama."

Alabama! How come he didn't know that? "The only residence in my files is the one in Buckhead. There's nothing about a house in Alabama."

"Well, I'm looking at the key right now."

"Where did you get it?"

She hesitated before answering. "I can't say."

Gina Harris. Who else? he thought. But why hadn't she told him about the place? "Vanessa, I need you to be frank with me for a minute. I need to know everything you know about Christopher, and I mean everything. I just . . ."

"I told you I didn't know a lot about him. Even less than I thought I knew."

"What do you mean by that?"

"Nothing. Look, I've got the key, and if you don't want to go check it out, I'll do it myself."

"Leave the detective work to the police." She was a piece of work. And to think he missed seeing her.

"I would, but you guys move too slow. Christopher's been dead two weeks, and what are the police doing? Dragging their heels. You've got no suspect, no evidence, nothing. Did the autopsy report even come back yet? Not that I expected more from the police, but I thought you were different. You seem more caring, like you really want to help."

How did this call get so out of hand? "Vanessa, stop and breathe for a minute. I do want to help. And you have no idea how much work has gone into this case." Who did this woman think she was? He was going to tell her about the autopsy, but not now.

"But you didn't know about his home in Alabama?"

"No, I didn't. And there's something else I didn't know until this evening."

"What's that?"

"That you know who killed Christopher Harris."

"What! Who told you that?"

"I can't say." He mocked her earlier words.

"It's a lie. I don't know what type of game you're playing, but if I knew I would have told you. So I'm going to Alabama tomorrow. But that's okay. Don't you worry about it. I'll go check it out myself. Tell you what. Why don't I let *you* know what I find out. Who knows? I might be able to solve this one for you."

Eric shook his head, a little too upset to speak for a moment. This woman was beautiful, but impossible.

"Detective, if there's nothing else, I need to go. I have a long drive in the morning."

"No, that's all. Enjoy the ride."

"I'm sure I will."

He jumped as the phone slammed down in his ear.

She had an uncanny way of turning everything around and upside down. He pulled the file on Christopher Harris and scanned the notes about a home in Alabama. Again he got up to leave, thinking about Vanessa on his way out. She was going to give him an ulcer before this was all over with.

Eight

Vanessa ran around Saturday morning getting everything she needed for the drive to Alabama. She didn't want to go by herself, but if it meant finding a clue as to what Christopher was working on, she'd go.

After a quick breakfast of oatmeal and fruit she threw on a pair of jeans, a T-shirt, and grabbed a lightweight jacket. Inside her purse, she tucked a notepad and a small tape recorder, just in case she needed them.

The bright morning sun hit her the minute she opened the front door. She pulled her shades out, and put them on. She'd left her car parked in the drive after gassing up earlier.

"It's about time you came out of there."

Vanessa looked up at Eric sitting on the hood of her car. "What the . . . ?" She stopped and looked at him in disbelief. Deep down, she was glad to see him, excited even, but she'd never admit it.

"Have you lost your mind or what?" she asked, walking to the car.

"Nope, I changed my mind. I can't let you drive down there alone."

She pointed at her car. "I meant sitting on the hood of my car. You're gonna dent it. How much do you weigh anyway?" She strolled over to the driver's side and opened the door.

Eric jumped down from the hood and dusted off the

rear of his jeans. "Not enough to hurt your car. If I do, I'll fix it." He walked over to her and stood on the other side of the opened car door.

When he'd jumped off the hood, she'd almost dropped her car keys. She gazed over his form in those jeans. Nice fit. In fact, they fit too well. At least they weren't those baggy, off-your-butt jeans the younger men were wearing.

"So you want to tag along on my journey?" she asked, throwing her purse into the backseat.

"Or I can drive, and you can tag along with me. Whichever you like, but I can't let you go alone."

"I don't see why not. The police aren't interested in the truth. I know you don't have time for things like this."

"Vanessa, this is my day off. I've chosen to drive to Alabama with you, so don't tell me I'm not interested. I told you yesterday, I think you know more than you're telling me. Maybe you aren't aware of it, but regardless, I think you can help this case."

"And you came to this conclusion based on a phone call yesterday, right?"

"That's right. The caller said he knew who killed Christopher. He said—ask his partner. So until I can solve this case one way or the other, I'm going to stick with you like a puppy to his owner."

"That call could have been a hoax."

"Like the letter?"

She narrowed her eyes at him. He wasn't so sure she hadn't written that letter herself. She could see it in his eyes. One minute he looked as if he liked her, the next he looked as if he suspected her of something.

"Eric, you've been sitting out here in the sun too long."

He laughed. "So how far away is this place? And

whose car are we taking? Yours or mine?" He rubbed his palms together.

"The whole trip should take about nine hours. Let's take my car. Get in." She got into the car and unlocked the doors. Eric walked around the front of the car and her eyes followed him every step of the way. For one brief moment he reminded her of Tony. Thank God he wasn't.

Eric had gotten into the car and said something while she was daydreaming. "I'm sorry. What did you say?"

"Looks like we'll have nice weather for the ride. I bet the weatherman wakes up happy, knowing he always has something to look forward to."

"Yeah, that one day he'll get it right," she said sarcastically.

Eric threw back his head and let out a hearty laugh. "You're something else, you know that?"

"Well, it's true. They never get it right."

"Yeah, I guess it's a tough job. Do you have the address and good directions?" He buckled himself in.

She did the same. "Of course I have the directions. What do you think I'm going to do, jump in the car and try to find the place when I get there?" She started the car.

When he didn't respond, she knew he was looking at her. She pulled out trying not to look in his direction. Once they were onto the interestate, she reached over and turned up the radio.

Eric turned it back down. "I'd like to talk to you for a minute."

"You can't hear with the radio on?"

"Not with it blasting. That's why I turned it down."

"Hmm . . . touchy, aren't we?"

"No, but you are. And we need to talk about that." He turned and faced her, throwing his hand behind her headrest.

"I'm not touchy." She glanced at him and caught him looking down at her jeans.

"Then what's up with you? Every time I'm around you, all you do is get smart with me."

"I do not. It bothers me the way you guys—"

"What, 'you guys'? Since I've been assigned to this case, what other detectives have you talked with?"

Now she wished she'd left him standing in front of her house. She didn't want to argue with him. "You're the only person I've talked with."

"Then, what's with all this, you guys get this wrong, you guys get that wrong? Why are you hatin' on the police so much?"

"I'm not hatin'."

"I have to tell you, I feel like you're taking something out on me . . . wooo." Eric reached out and braced himself against the dashboard when Vanessa slammed on the brakes.

"I'm sorry, but that car stopped short."

"No problem." He waited until they were moving clearly in traffic again before continuing. "Do you want to tell me what I'm being punished for? And I know it has more to do with a simple altercation between you and some cop."

She looked out her side window, wishing she could avoid this conversation. He was already making her nervous. She exhaled and decided to let him know about Tony, and then he'd understand why she felt the way she did.

"Do you really want to hear this?" she asked, biting her lip.

Eric crossed his arms over his chest. "I can't wait."

"I used to date a cop. He mistreated me so I tried to have him arrested. Big mistake. They treated me like some crazy woman. No matter what, he was right, and

I was wrong. That's why I say you guys all stick together."

"Sounds bad. I'm sorry. But I promise all policemen aren't alike. I don't know what kind of a cop he was, but I'm not him."

"No, but you still play by the same code of silence."

Eric uncrossed his arms and ran his hands down the front of his jeans. Vanessa knew she'd hit a chord with him.

"That's a subject I'd rather not discuss, but that should have had nothing to do with your ex-boyfriend being arrested, or suspended, if he deserved it. Being a cop doesn't excuse you from being a decent person."

"Well, it worked for him." She'd turned away, but glanced back at the road in time to see the brake lights in front of her glaring. She stepped on her brakes and stopped within a few inches of a new Infiniti Q45.

"Okay, this much traffic on a Saturday morning means there's a serious accident up ahead."

"Say, ah, why don't you let me take over?" Eric suggested after releasing his imaginary passenger-side brakes. His hand gripped the front dashboard.

Vanessa couldn't help but laugh. "What's wrong? You think I'm going to get us killed?"

"No, not at all. But maybe I distracted you. If you let me drive, we can talk about the case at the same time."

"Oh, so now I can't talk and drive at the same time?" She didn't take her eyes off the road, but traffic stopped again and she had to tap her brakes.

She glanced over at Eric who was smiling at her. "Traffic's horrible."

They laughed together. Vanessa put on her turning signal and maneuvered her way over to the shoulder. When she stopped, she told Eric, "I'm not letting you drive because I can't do two things at once—because I can. I'm letting you drive because traffic is ridiculous, and I don't want to get road rage on somebody out here with a detective in the car with me."

He unbuckled his seat belt. "Whatever your reason, I don't mind driving." He got out and walked around to the driver's side.

She climbed over into the passenger seat and was all buckled up by the time he got in. He adjusted everything he needed, then pulled back out into traffic, which was grinding to a halt.

Now Eric had a better understanding of where Vanessa was coming from. He couldn't take back what had happened to her, but he could try to restore her faith in policemen. He wanted her to know he was there for her, to protect her.

They continued to talk about traffic, the city, the Braves, the Hawks, and whatever else came to mind.

Eric pulled alongside a restored Thunderbird.

"Now that's sweet," he commented.

Vanessa glanced at the car. "What's so sweet about that old thing?"

He turned to her as if he'd been hit in the arm. "You don't know what you're looking at. That's a 1955 Ford Thunderbird with portholes. That's a classic."

"Yeah, but it's so old," she replied.

Eric shook his head as he eased off the brakes. "Do you know how much that car is worth?"

"Now or before he restored it?"

"Now."

"Oh, I'd guess about thirty or so thousand dollars. Am I close?"

"Close." He held up an index finger. "Right now, he could get over fifty thousand easy. The parts aren't that hard to come by, but they're expensive."

"How do you know?"

"I've got a 1966 Lincoln Continental convertible with suicide doors that I've begun restoring. It's going to take me some time to complete because the parts are so expensive."

"Is it hard work?"

"It's more time-consuming, but I love it. And it takes patience, which fortunately I have plenty of."

"So, do you go to car shows and stuff like that?"

"Yep. I've got a den full of restoration books and magazines. I'm always looking for old parts."

"Where did you get that from? Does your dad like old cars?"

"Not really. I don't know who my love for old cars came from. My dad was a detective for the Lexington police force. Most of his spare time was spent at church, or raising three wild men."

"Is that why you wanted to be a cop? To follow in your father's footsteps?"

"Yeah, I guess. I wanted to make the old man proud. My brother Michael's in law enforcement, too."

"Where's your family? Here in Georgia?"

"No, Lexington, Kentucky. Except for my youngest brother—he's a plant manager at Toyota in Richmond."

"No girls?"

He shook his head. "Not a one."

"Man, that must have been hell for your mother. I can't imagine four men in the house at the same time."

"It probably was pretty rough, but she handled it. My mom's a tough cookie. She works for the Lexington Board of Education, but my dad's retired."

"What was it like growing up in your household?"

What was this? Twenty Questions? Eric realized how he'd been doing all the talking, and didn't like being the center of attention. It wasn't like him to open his mouth and spill out so much personal information.

"That's enough about me. I want to know more about this feisty woman sitting next to me." He glanced at her.

After being stuck in accident traffic for almost three hours, they left the metro Atlanta area. Traffic cleared out. An overturned eighteen-wheeler and two smashed cars sat on the shoulder. They seemed to not have noticed the time at all.

"I'm not feisty," she responded, blushing.

"Sure you are. Come on, tell me something about yourself. Are you originally from Georgia?"

"No, I was born in New York. We lived in Manhattan until I was about five. Then my parents divorced, so we moved in with my grandmother on Long Island."

"You don't talk like a New Yorker. I don't detect a strong accent."

"That's what everyone tells me." She shrugged. "I don't know. I didn't move here until after college. My sister followed, and my mother wasn't too far behind her. And I thought that woman would never leave New York."

"Where's your grandmother? She stayed?"

"She passed away years ago when I was in high school."

"So, your whole family followed you to Georgia?"

"Just about. My father still lives there. He remarried years after the divorce."

"Sounds like your family's pretty close."

"Very. My mom remarried a few months after moving here. My sister's a carbon copy of her. I'm more like my father."

"Do you get along with your mother's husband?"

"At first it was a struggle. But now we're all pretty good friends. He's a good man."

As the hours passed, they continued out of Georgia and into Alabama, getting better acquainted. The more Vanessa talked, the more Eric liked her. She was so down-to-earth. He'd met a lot of beautiful women in Atlanta, but so many of them were busy pretending to be something they weren't, or were looking for men to take care of them. Vanessa didn't strike him that way.

"So who'd you get your height from—your mother or father?"

"Both I guess. My mom's about five-seven, and my father's a little over six feet."

"My next question is pretty typical."

"I know, and the answer is yes. I played basketball all through school. I went to college on a basketball scholarship."

Eric smiled at her and chuckled. "So I'm looking at a real athlete. What's your average?"

"I carried my own. I averaged about twenty-two points."

"Yeah?" he asked, surprised. "That's pretty good. I'll have to get you out on the court sometimes. See if you've still got that average."

"Oh, you want to challenge me?"

He grinned at her and shook his head. "I played a little ball myself. I didn't get a basketball scholarship though. I played baseball."

"Well, now, we do have something in common," She smiled at him, crossing her arms. She knew there was something she liked about this man.

"Do you still play?" he asked.

"Every chance I get. It's a good way to stay in shape."

He looked over at her, taking in every in-shape inch of her. "Yeah, and I see it pays off."

"Look out!" she screamed, staring ahead.

Nine

Eric jerked up just in time to notice a red car pulling out of a gas station, and heading right toward them. He swerved to keep the car from hitting them, then lost control. The back of the car slid to the left. He fought to straighten the wheel. A second later, they were headed off the side of the road. Ahead was a cliff.

Vanessa held on to the door handle with one hand and gripped the armrest with the other. Her breathing quickened as her heartbeat raced along with the car. She heard Eric swearing. Bracing herself, she closed her eyes. She had no idea what was over the cliff. She didn't know if they would flip over, hit a tree, live or die.

Then the car stopped, and Eric touched her leg.

"Vanessa, are you okay?" he asked in a protective tone.

Paralyzed with fear, she opened her eyes and looked around. They were alive. "Uh-huh. I think I'm okay."

Ahead of her was nothing but grass. To the right—a drop-off.

"Come on, get out."

Following him, she unbuckled her seat belt and opened the door. Her car was sitting on a bed of rocks. She jumped out of the car and ran around to the driver's side. Eric grabbed her hand and together they ran up the hill to the side of the road.

Once they reached the top, Vanessa looked back down

the cliff at her car sitting inches from the drop-off to a ravine. A fall that would have killed them had the car gone over into it.

"Damn." Eric looked up and down the highway. A black Corvette had pulled over into the parking lot of the restaurant next door. Eric ran toward the car.

A short stocky white man talking on a cell phone got out of the car. "I got some of it," he called out to Eric.

"Did you see who ran us off the road?" Eric asked, as he reached the Corvette.

"Sort of. It looked like a big dude. I got a piece of the tag, and I can describe the car. I'm calling the sheriff right now."

"Let's see what you got." Eric took the paper the young man held out.

The restaurant door opened and a few patrons came out and stood in the doorway to see what was going on. "Is everybody all right?" one woman called out.

Eric turned to look back at Vanessa. She stood looking down the hill. He walked over and put his hand on her shoulder. "You doing okay?"

She shook her head. "I can't believe it." She looked down at herself. "No blood, no pain, nothing. But I'm shaking like a leaf, and my heart feels like it's about to explode."

He took her hands in his, caressing them, then pulled her into his arms. "We're okay, thank God."

"Is she hurt?" another voice called out from the restaurant.

Eric turned to the people standing in the doorway. "No, she's fine. She's just shook up," he said, looking down into Vanessa's eyes.

"We called the sheriff. He'll be here in a minute," the woman continued.

"Thank you," Eric called back.

"Do you folks need to go to the hospital?" the stocky man asked after walking over to Eric and Vanessa.

"Thanks, but we're okay. I just can't believe that car saw us go over the cliff like that and kept going."

"Yeah, and he sped up after he passed. That's why I couldn't see the plates. He was going too fast. Driving like a madman."

"Well, I appreciate you calling the sheriff for us."

"Sure, man, no problem. I'll just be over here in the car so I can tell them what I saw."

Eric took his arms from Vanessa to shake the man's hand. He didn't go too far, and still held on to her hand. She squeezed his hand, not wanting to let it go. She hadn't wanted him to stop hugging her. When he did, her body shook. She looked at the people by the restaurant and at the gas station, across from the ravine, staring at them.

"Good. Here comes the sheriff. I'm going to talk to the officer and we'll see if we can't get a tow truck to get the car out." Eric let go of Vanessa's hand and together they walked over to the sheriff's car pulling into the restaurant lot. The siren wasn't on, but the lights were flashing. The minute he exited the car, Eric identified himself as a Fulton County Detective.

Vanessa saw Eric pull out his badge and show him his weapon. She hadn't even realized he had a gun on him. Vanessa let Eric do most of the talking.

The officer took all the information from her, Eric, and the stocky white guy who saw the whole thing. He called another officer to the scene and off he went, supposedly after the car that ran them off the road.

An hour later, a tow truck pulled up and a tall dark-haired man with an old greasy baseball cap and overalls to match stepped out.

He exchanged words with Eric and the deputy sheriff before walking over to look down at the car. Vanessa stood next to him, glancing at his belly hanging over his belt.

"Is that your car?" he asked.

"Yeah."

"You couldn't have found a better place to park it?"

Vanessa looked up to see a smile on his big round face with yellowing teeth, and realized he was joking with her. She laughed for the first time since the accident. It relieved a little of the tension. "Believe me, it wasn't by choice."

Eric walked over and they discussed how they were going to get the car out. Vanessa felt so helpless.

"Well, we could yank her out from behind, or . . ."

"Sir, do you have to yank anything?" she asked, thinking of her poor car.

"Call me Jerry." He extended his hand and shook hers and Eric's for the first time.

"I'm just messin' with ya. We'll hook her up and ease her out of there. You've probably got some damage underneath. I'll take a look." He started down the hill.

"Come on down and take a look with me, fella," he called back to Eric.

Eric followed him down the hill. They walked around the car, inspecting and pointing.

Vanessa looked at her watch. Where had the time gone? Sean said Luverne was about a three-hour drive. After being stuck in Atlanta, they'd driven an additional three hours, but hadn't made it. So it was farther away. She hoped the car wasn't damaged too badly, so they would be able to continue the trip. She didn't see any dents.

"How's it look?" she called out.

Both men walked back up the hill. Eric was shaking his head. "Not good."

"Little lady, you've got some motor damage there. I don't think you'll be driving out of here today." He turned, looking back down the hill as he pulled up his baseball cap and scratched his head.

"You're kidding."

"Is there a good garage in town?" Eric asked.

"Sure is. Brookwell's is the best garage in all the surrounding counties. You're in luck."

Eric turned to Vanessa. "Good for us."

"Well, I'll pull her out and we can get on over to the garage."

Once the car was hooked up onto the tow truck, Vanessa and Eric climbed in with Jerry. He turned the radio station on to the local country-Western station.

"Where were you folks headed anyway?" Jerry asked.

"We were on our way to Luverne, Alabama," Eric responded.

"Nice town. I been there. Got people there?"

Eric looked down at Vanessa. He had his arm around her shoulder, along the back of the seat. "No, we're going for a little business," Eric added.

"I hope you make it over there. Brookwell's good, but I don't think he'll have you out of there tonight," Jerry stated.

Vanessa looked around the garage with whistle-white walls and clean-swept floors. Large birdcages with colorful parrots were in the lobby and garage area. The owner, James Brookwell, and his wife, Anita, offered them everything from soda to snacks.

After Vanessa used the phone to call her insurance company, Eric broke the news to her that it would take a few weeks to fix the car.

"What are we going to do?" she asked, standing with her arms crossed.

He looked down at his watch. "We can rent a car and keep going if you want. We're not that far away. Or we can go back to Atlanta. I can drive you back in a few weeks to pick up your car."

"I don't want to go back."

"Mr. Daniels." Anita worked the front counter.

Eric turned from Vanessa to Anita. "Yes."

"I'm afraid I've got some bad news."

Eric walked over to the counter and Vanessa followed him, looked into her purse to see how much cash she had on her. She hadn't planned on any unexpected stops. She had twenty-five dollars and a credit card.

"Wallace, who runs the car-rental place isn't in. He closed up early today."

"So we can't rent a car?" Eric questioned in disbelief.

Anita frowned and shook her head. "I'm afraid not. But if you want, we can call over to Creek County Rentals and see if they've got any cars."

"Could you please?" Vanessa spoke up. What was she going to do without a car?

Eric stood there scratching behind his ear as he pulled out his cell phone.

Vanessa tried not to listen to his call, but couldn't help it because he was so close. He called a police friend to see if they knew anyone in the area. After he hung up, he stood there cracking his knuckles.

"Any good news?" she asked, regarding the call.

He shook his head. "Afraid not."

"Don't you have any police connections to get us out of here? Flip your badge at someone. I thought you guys all stuck together."

"There you go with that again. Like I said, sorry I don't know anyone who lives in this area. We're on our own."

Anita cleared her throat to get their attention.

"Yes? What did you find out?" Eric eagerly asked.

"Bobby said they don't have no more cars right now. Something's going on over at the local high school and the kids have rented all the cars. Actually, their parents rent the cars, but he don't have any more."

"All the cars?" Eric asked, astounded.

"That's what he said. But he don't have that many to start with." Anita shrugged.

"That's unbelievable," he stated, staring at her. "Can you try another place?"

"I could, but Montgomery is miles away, and they don't deliver cars this far."

"You folks might as well make yourself comfortable. Don't look like you're going anywhere tonight." Jerry added his two cents.

Vanessa stared at the back of Eric's head until he turned to look at her. There was no way she was going to spend the night in this little country town. She wasn't prepared. No clean underclothes, no toothbrush—no way.

"Looks like we're stuck," Eric said.

"Honey, y'all might as well check into the Luverne Motel for the night. We'll even have Wallace bring you a car over in the morning, then you can continue your trip."

"Are you sure you don't have a car here we could rent from you?" Vanessa asked in a desperate plea.

"Honey, we repair 'em, we don't rent 'em."

"I can't believe there's not another car rental place in this whole town," Vanessa commented in a harsh tone.

"Believe it, honey. Wallace is it."

The door to the garage area opened and James Brookwell came in. "Mr. Daniels, I just talked to Officer Brown and he's coming by to talk to you again about the accident."

"Did they catch the person who ran us off the road?" Eric asked.

James shrugged. "He didn't say. Just said to let you

know he was on his way over, and not to leave before he gets here."

"Well, in that case," Jerry said, standing, "I've got to get back to work. I'll let you folks ride over to the motel with Officer Brown." He smiled and winked at Vanessa.

She turned to Anita who was smiling, then to Eric. How on earth did she get herself into situations like this?

"Thank you. We'll catch Officer Brown and get a room for the night," he told Jerry, then turned to Anita. "And if you can have Wallace bring us a car in the morning, I'd appreciate it."

Vanessa opened her mouth to protest, but didn't get a word out before Eric continued while looking at her. "We can check into the motel for tonight and continue our trip tomorrow. You didn't have any plans for Sunday, did you?"

"Uh, church and dinner at my mom's, but . . ."

"You'll miss church, but we'll be back in time for dinner. Then it's all set. We'll get a room for the night."

Ten

"You folks might want to walk over to the Roadhouse Grill as soon as you check in. It's across the street from the motel. Unfortunately, it's gonna be the closest place to you, and it also happens to be a hangout for the teens on Saturday nights," Officer Brown informed them as they drove down the main street.

"I could use a toothbrush," Vanessa said, looking first at Eric, then out the window for a drugstore.

"Yeah. Think we can make a quick stop?" Eric asked.

"No problem."

After a stop at the local dollar store, they continued to the Luverne Motel. Vanessa frowned as they pulled up to the rusty-looking gray building with falling curtains hanging in the windows. Eric looked back at her and smiled.

"Well, here we are." Officer Brown drove the squad car up to the front door of the motel, got out, and opened the passenger door for Vanessa.

"Is this the only motel with vacancies?" she asked looking at the MOT L sign as it flickered.

"It's the only motel, period. But Helen will treat you nice. Y'all go on in and make yourselves comfortable."

Eric talked to Officer Brown for a few minutes before the policeman drove off.

Vanessa looked up at the motel, which reminded her of a seedy place where you might find prostitutes or drifters, like in a movie. Eric took Vanessa's hand as they entered the motel.

"What's he doing about catching the car who caused us to wreck?"

"They've been trying to catch him. Don't worry, I'll take care of it."

With her bag of Lysol, toothbrush, and toothpaste in hand, she followed him into the lobby. She couldn't believe this was happening. One minute they were driving and getting to know each other, the next they were checking into a motel.

"How can I help you folks?" the clerk behind the desk asked, smacking on her chewing gum. Behind her was a radio playing a Randy Travis tune.

"We'd like to get two rooms for the night." Eric reached into his wallet and pulled out his credit card.

Vanessa pulled her wallet out of her purse to get her credit card.

"Don't." Eric stopped her. "I got this."

The clerk scrolled through her computer screen shaking her head. "Well, now, looks like we've got one room left." She looked from Eric to Vanessa. "You want that?"

"One room! The parking lot's not even full." Vanessa didn't understand how this dump could be full.

"Well, you see," the clerk explained between smacks, "we're doin' a little remodeling, so only half the motel is available."

Eric looked at his watch, then at Vanessa. "What do you think?"

"I think not." She shoved her wallet back into her purse.

He turned back to the clerk. "The room has double beds, right?"

She looked up at her computer screen again, then over at Eric. She shook her head. "One queen."

"Just a minute," Eric said to the clerk before pulling Vanessa aside.

"Look, we don't really have a choice. It's this motel or outside on the street. You can have the bed and I'll sleep in a chair."

She crossed her arms and stood defying him. "I bet if you offered her some money she'd find another room."

He lowered his head and glared at her. "Vanessa, where do you think we are? This is Alabama. You've been watching too many movies."

She let out a heavy sigh. "Okay, get the key."

He walked over to the clerk to pay for the room.

Vanessa watched him, shaking her head. *I can't believe this,* she thought while tapping her foot on the carpet. For a moment, she thought about calling Betty to come pick them up. Then she remembered Betty and Harold had gone out of town. Since her mother didn't own a car, but drove her stepfather's, she was out of the question. But she had friends. Who did she know well enough to ask to come pick them up in a town three hours away, at seven-thirty on a Saturday night? Nobody.

"Room 219." Eric held up a large key holder and key, with 219 written in big bold black letters.

She smiled at him. "Man, this is a small town. They don't have swipe cards for the door?"

Eric shook his head and scratched his temple. "Come on, I'm hungry. Let's grab some dinner."

After several loud, large, hauling trucks passed, they managed to cross the street to the Roadhouse Grill. The parking lot had a few souped-up compact cars and trucks with white teenagers hanging in the doorways playing loud rap music.

"Looks like we beat the crowd." Eric opened the door for Vanessa.

"Boy, they sure know how to live, don't they?"

"Oh, come on. Don't tell me you didn't enjoy cruising and parking when you were young?"

She stepped on something and kicked it from under her shoe. When she looked down, peanut shells were all over the floor. "If I did, I sure in hell don't remember it. We went to skating rinks and movie theaters."

They approached the hostess stand.

"Hello, folks. Smoking or nonsmoking?" the hostess asked, grabbing two menus and smiling up at them.The young white woman had red streaks in her hair and her tongue was pierced.

"Nonsmoking," Eric answered.

"What's this all over the floor?" Vanessa asked, knowing what it was, but not quite sure why they were there.

"Peanut shells." The hostess seated them at a both with a window view. "Your waiter will bring you a basket. After you open them, just throw the shells on the floor." She smiled as she placed their menus on the table.

Vanessa grinned at Eric. "Isn't that nice? Just throw them on the floor." She crinkled her nose. "So country."

They slid into the booth.

"Your waiter will be right with you. Enjoy."

"I'm sure we will," Vanessa said with a Southern drawl and a smile.

Eric wanted to burst out laughing, but he held it in. Vanessa was like no woman he had ever met. She was feisty, headstrong, and could be downright rude. But he liked her. Most of all, he liked the feistiness in her.

"Vanessa, you're something else, you know that?" He rested his forearms against the table with his fingers laced.

She set her purse to her side and turned to him. "What do you mean?"

"You can be quite difficult." He raised his left brow and grinned at her.

"I'm not difficult. I'm upset because we should be at

Christopher's right now looking for some evidence to prove his innocence."

"And to prove that you're not connected in any way."

She leaned forward and stared at him with squinted eyes. "Yes, I suppose that, too. But I'm doing this for his sister." Taking a breath, she sat back. "Somewhere in that house is proof he didn't steal anything, and the identity of whoever did. I can feel it. We've got to get there."

"This is just a temporary detour. If something's there, we'll find it."

"Why did you decide to come with me?" She leaned back, crossing her arms.

"The autopsy, the phone call, the family's insistence that it wasn't a suicide. Each one tells me I'd better take another look into this case." He didn't want to scare her by telling her he was now looking for a suspect.

"You're lying. You found something, didn't you?"

He shook his head. "Not yet. That's why I decided to tag along with you. You're going to lead me to something."

She didn't respond, but stared at him. Maybe she was trying to decide how much to tell him. Or if she should tell him anything at all.

"So let's eat and enjoy the detour," he said as the waiter walked up to take their order.

After dinner they walked back to the motel. Again they had to wait for the truck convoy to pass before crossing the street.

After climbing the stairs to room 219, Eric opened the door. The door seemed stuck. He gave it a hard shove, causing the curtains to blow back from the force. The smell of tobacco smoke reached out like menacing fingers and guided them into the dark dingy room.

Vanessa walked in behind Eric, holding her bag from

the local dollar store. Eric looked back with a twisted smile.

"Well, this is our room for the night."

"It ain't the Taj Mahal, huh?" She walked in, fanning the air, then set her bag down and pulled out the can of Lysol. With her nose turned up she walked into the bathroom, inspecting the orange-brownish carpet along the way. She turned the fan on and proceeded to spray everything down.

Eric stood in the doorway. "What are you doing?"

"Do you know how many people have been in this bathroom? I can't even wash my hands in here until I've disinfected it thoroughly." She pulled back the shower curtain and sprayed inside. She walked back out into the claustrophobically small room and sprayed the bedspread.

"Hold on. Don't get so heavy-handed with that stuff." Coughing, Eric walked over to open the door. He held it open.

"Yeah, let a little air in. Does this place have air-conditioning?"

"It should. Right now I'm trying not to die from Lysol poisoning." He slid out of his jacket and threw it across a chair in front of the window.

Vanessa set the can on the dresser. "I'm sorry. I didn't mean to overdo it. I saw this report on *60 Minutes* about how unclean motel and hotel rooms are. You wouldn't believe the amount of dried—" She stopped herself and looked up at him. "Never mind."

"This is going to be some trip, you know that?" Eric laughed as he closed the door.

"Why do you say that?" she asked as she proceeded to open all the drawers of the dresser, peeking inside.

Eric grabbed the television remote from the table, pulled out a chair, and sat down. He clicked on the television mounted high on the wall. "What are you doing now?"

"I'm just making sure past guests didn't leave anything behind. Like anything disgusting."

"I think you watch too much television." He flicked the channel over to a basketball game.

"Maybe so." She walked over and pulled the bedspread all the way back. Then she pulled back the sheet and sat on the corner of the bed.

Eric stared at her for a few minutes before commenting. "You sprayed that bedspread then turned it down. Why?"

"I'm not going to sit on that. People have sex on the top of bedspreads, you know."

"Oh." He nodded his head. "Right." He'd like to be a part of those "people" right about now.

For the next half hour they sat watching a basketball game. Vanessa was as much into the game as Eric. She got up and walked over to hang her jacket up.

With her jacket off, Eric admired her as she looked in the mirror in the dressing area. His attention was no longer on the game. Her jeans hugged her rear end and traveled smoothly down her long legs. He wanted to walk over and put his hands into her back pockets. He wanted to feel underneath her jeans, to hold what filled them so completely.

"Who's winning?" she asked, coming back and taking the seat across the table from him.

"New York, I think." He blinked and looked back up at the television. However, his mind still wasn't on the game. Here he sat in a motel room with a beautiful black woman whom he wanted to make love to, but he didn't dare try. He wasn't sure if the attraction was mutual or not, although he'd seen a look in her eyes from time to time that told him it was.

What was he thinking about? She was a part of the

case. He didn't want to make the mistake of getting involved again with a woman on a case and possibly causing her harm.

He had to get his mind off her if he was going to make it through the night. During the next commercial break, he stood and walked over to the bed. "I'm going to make a quick phone call."

"Okay. The bathroom should be safe now. I need to freshen up." She went into the bathroom while he was on the phone.

"Man, I don't believe you. You go out for evidence and wind up in a motel with this woman. You lucky son of a—"

"Hey, man. I told you we had a wreck. This wasn't planned. In the morning I'll see what I find. Did you talk to the chief for me?"

"Yeah, but he said to talk to the primary. Better catch him first thing Monday. I think he wants you to close this thing up."

"Damn, I was afraid of that."

"Where's she at right now?" Harper asked.

"In the bathroom." Eric paced back and forth in the small area. He heard water running in the bathroom and was assured she wasn't on her way out.

"Before you take off, I need you to look into something for me," Eric said.

"Sure, what's up?"

Eric reached into his pocket and pulled out a slip of paper. "I've got a partial car tag I need checked out."

Vanessa turned off the water and dried her face as she stared back at herself in the mirror. How was she going to sleep tonight? Where would he sleep tonight? His long body would never fit into those chairs like he suggested. And no way could she sleep in bed next to him.

All she'd done since they left the restaurant was run those questions through her mind. She thought about being with him, lying next to him, touching him.

When she walked out of the bathroom, Eric was stretched out across the bed watching the game.

She tried not to look as flushed as she felt. "I'd better make a call, too. I need to let my sister know what happened and where I'm at."

"Don't forget whom you're with." He rose up on one elbow.

"That'll be the first thing I tell her." She grabbed the phone from the nightstand and pulled it over to the table. He turned back to the game.

Vanessa dialed Betty's cell phone and talked in a low whisper, filling her in on the details of the accident. Before hanging up, she promised to call her first thing in the morning.

After the game was over, Vanessa took off her shoes and crawled up into the seat. She flipped through the channels.

"I know you're sleepy, so we might as well hit the sack. You can have the bed, and I'll pull these chairs together." Eric kicked off his shoes, then took off his shirt and hung it on back of the chair.

Vanessa nodded, in and out of sleep. The air conditioner wasn't good enough and she wanted to climb out of her jeans, but she didn't dare. Suddenly there was a loud knock at the door.

Eric jumped up and peeked out the curtain first. "Who is it?" he asked with his ear to the door. He looked back at Vanessa edging up the bed. He crossed the room to his jacket and pulled out his gun. Holding it down, he returned to the door, jerking it open. He stepped out and looked around.

Vanessa could hear some kids laughing and screaming in the distance.

Eric walked back in, closed and locked the door. "It was just some kids. Saturday night. They must be having a party."

"Is that necessary?" she asked, pointing to his gun. "It makes me feel like you're some type of bodyguard."

"Tonight, I am your bodyguard," he said before putting the gun in the dresser drawer and sitting back down.

She grabbed the sheet and squeezed it close to her. "My body needs more than a little guarding right now," she mumbled under her breath.

"What?" he asked, turning around.

"Nothing. Look, I'm not sleepy. So what do we do?"

Eric looked out the window once more before turning to Vanessa. "I've got a few ideas, but we're better off with whatever you've got in mind. You wouldn't happen to have a deck of cards in your purse?"

"No, I don't. But maybe you could tell me what you know about Christopher's case. It might help tomorrow." She had to think of something to get his T-shirt and muscles off her mind. If they talked business, she would get caught up in the conversation and not think about sex.

"You know I can't do that. Why don't we find a good movie instead?" He put his feet up in an attempt to make himself comfortable.

His legs were too long, and the back of the chair wasn't high enough. He fidgeted in the chair, trying to get comfortable. Frustrated, he pulled his legs back and kicked the chair away.

Vanessa detected his frustration as she pulled the sheet over herself and propped up on a pillow, watching television. He looked so funny. A big man in two little chairs. She wanted to laugh, but continued to watch his efforts.

He slouched down in the seat, hoping to make it a

little more comfortable, but it wasn't. Maybe he'd stretch out on the floor. One look at the soiled orange-brownish carpet, and he changed his mind. He looked over at Vanessa lying alone in that queen-size bed.

"Can you check the air again?" she asked. "It's stuffy in here."

"I did already. It's up as high as it will go. Get out of those jeans if you're so hot."

"No, I'm sleeping in them."

He got up and moved over to the bed.

"Then you won't mind if I crash on this side. That damned chair is killing my back. I might have hurt it a little in the accident." He looked back at Vanessa fully clothed.

"What are you doing? You can't sleep here." Her eyes revealed her anxiety.

"I have to. I told you, those chairs are killing me." He stretched out, and lay his head on the pillow with his back to her. "Just like your jeans are probably cutting off your circulation."

"No, they aren't."

"Look, feel free to take something off. I won't bite. You don't have to sleep in all your clothes. It's hot as hell in here."

"I can feel a little air," she commented.

Eric sat up and turned to face her. They stared at each other a few seconds before breaking out into laughter. Eric fell back onto the pillow.

"It is hot and stuffy in here. I must look crazy fully dressed with this sheet pulled up."

He reached over and wiped her forehead. "Not to mention you're perspiring."

The back of his hand moved slowly across her forehead and seductively down the side of her face. She let go of the sheet. Her body temperature rose even higher.

She jumped up from bed. "Look, we're adults, right?"

He rose up on one elbow. "Right."

"So it should be okay for me to take off a few things and climb under the sheet without worrying about you taking advantage of me," Vanessa said, but her tone wasn't quite so convincing.

Eric sat up all the way and held up his right hand. "Ms. Benton, you have my word of honor as a gentleman that I won't touch you, or even look at you. You can climb under the cover and I'll stay on top. This is one detective you won't have to worry about. Scout's honor."

She gave him a sideways glance. "Are you going to take off your jeans?"

He lowered his hand and his head and gave a low seductive laugh.

"What's so funny? It's hot in here, I asked an innocent question."

He looked back up at her with an enticing smile. "I don't think I'd better."

She turned around so he couldn't see her blush. She sat back down on the bed and began unbuttoning her jeans. When she looked back at him, he'd already turned around facing the window. She slid out of her jeans, threw them at the foot of the bed, and jumped under the covers.

"Eric?"

"Yeah."

"Thanks for everything today."

"No problem."

"And thanks for being such a gentleman about tonight."

"Sure, but I have to confess something."

"What?" she asked, turning her head slightly.

"I was never a Boy Scout."

Eleven

Vanessa lay there, staring at the television, watching, but not really watching the picture. All she could think about was the man lying next to her. The last time she lay this close to a man, she made sure he went home before daybreak. Eric would be there in the morning when she woke, like a lover.

A faint snore came from his side of the bed. She sat up and looked around at him. "I sure hope you don't get any louder than that," she said to him although he was asleep. "Damn, I knew I wasn't going to get any sleep tonight." She fell back on the pillow, causing the bed to bounce.

Eric stirred as he repositioned himself, but never woke up.

Minutes later, still unable to sleep, Vanessa flipped through the cable stations looking for something worth watching. She stopped at a man and woman sharing a passionate kiss. They circled a bedroom before ripping off each other's clothes a piece at a time, then fell onto the bed somehow without parting lips and began tumbling about. The scene looked more like assault than passion, she thought. She could show them how to do it right.

No. Sleep, sleep. Go to sleep, she chanted. *Don't think of him, don't think of sex, don't think of anything but sleep.* Sheep! Yes, she'd try counting sheep. She started fast then slowed.

As soon as her body was totally relaxed and drifting off to sleep, a loud blaring sound came from outside.

Simultaneously, she and Eric jumped up in bed.

"What—what's going on?" Eric turned to Vanessa. "What was that?" he asked, his eyes open wide.

When she'd jumped up, the sheet had fallen around her waist. Her T-shirt was rolled up, and her midriff was exposed. She looked around the room startled. "A train. It sounded like a train."

The horn of trucks going down the road sounded again. This time a few horns were blown as they roared through.

"Trucks," they said at the same time.

"It sounds like a trains rolling right outside that door," Vanessa commented.

"Yeah, it's loud as hell." Eric noticed her exposed skin. "You still hot?" he asked.

In more ways than one, she wanted to say, but bit her lip. Instead, she nodded her head.

"Want me to go get a bucket of ice?"

"And do what with it?" she asked, giving him a no-you-don't look.

He shrugged. "Whatever you want. Cool you off, eat it."

"That won't cool me off. It just might have the opposite effect." She fell back on the bed.

Eric kept his distance and looked down at her. He was on fire, but didn't want to admit it to himself. He'd actually thought she might want to eat the ice. But he liked the way she thought.

"Want me to fan you?" he asked in his most seductive voice. Maybe she'd want that ice after all.

"No. Stay away from me."

"Can't take it, huh?" He fell back onto his pillow.

"Can't take what? I don't know what you're talking about."

"Sure you do. I see the way you look at me. Admit it, you want me." What the hell, he couldn't sleep now anyway. He might as well have some fun.

She popped up on her elbow. "What! You must be hallucinating."

"Don't be afraid to admit it. The feeling's mutual."

"Please"—she lowered herself back down—"don't flatter yourself."

They lay staring at the ceiling, bating each other for a while. Eric grew hotter and hotter with each comment. He fought the urge to turn around and pull her into his arms. He wanted to rip her top off and kiss her luscious round breasts. And it wasn't only her breasts that he wanted to taste. He wanted to do much more. . . .

"What do you mean you like me, too?" Vanessa asked.

Eric had forgotten he'd said it. "I'm just saying you're a beautiful attractive woman, aside from the fact that you sometimes drive me crazy." He turned his gaze from the ceiling and looked over at her. She was staring back at him.

"Thank you, I think."

From the little light coming through the crack in the curtains, he could see her eyes. Those soft brown eyes staring back at him, saying they wanted him as much as he wanted her. His pulse quickened at the same time the little angel on his shoulder shouted, *No.*

Forget it, he said, and leaned across the bed. He hoped she wouldn't turn away from him and she didn't.

The minute their lips touched, Eric knew he'd gone too far to turn back. He tasted her lips, her tongue, the sweetness that lingered inside of her. He started to bring his leg around when a blaring freight train roared at full blast, shaking the room.

The racket broke his concentration, and their kiss. Vanessa sat up holding on to the bed as if they'd been through an earthquake.

"Now was that a train?" she asked.

Eric eased off the bed and peeked out the window. He could see a herd of eighteen-wheelers rolling down the highway. "Trucks," he said, disheartened.

"That was one hell of a truck. I felt the room shake. Didn't you?"

He walked over to lie back down. "Yeah, it's a whole convoy of trucks. Looks like this place is on a truck route."

Vanessa turned around and looked at the clock radio. It was twelve-thirty-five. "It's late. I'd better try and get some sleep." She turned away from him and pulled the sheet back over on her.

"Yeah, we've got a busy day tomorrow." He adjusted himself and lay down, staring up at the ceiling. He was losing control. It wasn't good to get involved with her. Involvement on a case could only lead to trouble.

"Good night," she said softly.

"Good night."

Vanessa ran her finger across her lips. What the hell was she doing letting him kiss her? She was so hot, it didn't make sense. Maybe she should be ashamed of herself for lusting after him. But she wasn't. If he wasn't a detective, they might stand a chance. But he was. It didn't matter how good he kissed or did anything else for that matter, she wasn't going there again. Being involved with a cop was like walking a tightrope. She wasn't ready to join that club.

The next morning, Eric jumped up and hit the bathroom before Vanessa woke up. When he came out, he woke her then went to call about their rental car while she dressed in the bathroom.

He hadn't quite known what to say to Vanessa about his behavior last night, so he hadn't mentioned it. Besides, it was nothing more than a simple kiss. If she hadn't wanted him she would have pushed him away. But she didn't. If it hadn't been for those damned trucks, who knows what might have happened.

Talking with Officer Brown from a phone in the motel lobby, Eric found out there was no sign yet of the car that ran them off the road. He didn't mention the trace he'd started on his own. He had to make sure the accident wasn't connected to the case in any way.

Wallace brought over the promised rental car and after they completed some paperwork, they were on their way. Eric drove the Grand Am as they continued the trip to Luverne, Alabama.

They found the house on a country road. Eric pulled into the driveway, wrapped around to the back of the house.

Eric whistled. "Nice place. Your boy must have a little money. Looks like about three acres of land."

Vanessa eyed him sharply. "Since he's a man, he might make a little more than me. Then, too, we don't know how he invests his money." She pointed at Eric as if to say *Don't go there.*

Eric walked around to get the car door for Vanessa, but she'd already climbed out. "I already checked, and his investments aren't that deep."

She pulled out the door key. "He didn't take any money. And that's the last time I'm saying that."

They walked to the front door, she opened it, and they stepped inside. Eric closed the door behind them, as Vanessa ventured inside in awe of the place.

"My God, this place is out of sight."

"Expensive" is all Eric said as he looked around.

After seeing Gina's house, Vanessa should not have been surprised, but she had no idea Christopher had this much money. She walked all around checking everything out. The kitchen was spacious, with all up-to-date stainless-steel appliances. A huge island sat in the middle. Somebody did a lot of cooking in that kitchen. The adjoining dining room was huge and rich looking.

Eric found her standing at the back door looking out at the pool. "So Christopher had this place and his place in Atlanta?" he said in an insinuating tone.

Vanessa shook her head. She knew it looked bad.

"How do you suppose he could afford all this?"

"I know what you're getting at. But he shares this home with Sean, his lover."

"His lover?"

"Yeah, he was gay."

"How long have you known?"

She walked out onto the patio, followed by Eric, and sat in a chair under the umbrella. "I found out the other day when he gave me the key to this house." She set her purse on the patio table and put the house key inside.

"I thought his sister gave you the key."

"I never said that."

"No, you actually never said where you got the key. I just assumed it was his sister." He looked around at the pool area and the flowers and shrubs everywhere. "Well, that explains a few things."

"Like this big house? Maybe Sean is the one with all the money," she said.

"Yeah, and those privacy shrubs." He pointed at them before walking back inside. "Just like the ones in your backyard. Come on, we've got a job to do."

Vanessa followed him back inside. They found Christopher's office in the basement. There was a huge desk, a television, and bookcases full of books. Several boxes lined one wall as if he wasn't finished unpacking.

"I'm not sure what we're looking for. Do you have any idea?" Eric asked, looking over papers on Christopher's desk.

"Let's just say I'll know when I see it."

Eric stood in front of the bookshelf and picked up a picture frame. "Is this his boyfriend?"

Vanessa joined him. "Yeah, that's Sean." She picked up another picture of a small dog wearing sunglasses and a bandana around his neck. "And this is Ringo."

"He named his dog Ringo?"

"Yep. His best buddy." She looked up at Eric. "That much I did know about Christopher. He loved his dog. And now Sean takes care of him."

"Too bad Ringo can't talk. Maybe he could tell us what's going on."

"You're a cop. You don't need a dog. Sniff it out yourself."

"Okay, enough with the cop cracks. The minute you hear a strange noise out your back door you'll be looking for a cop."

She shrugged and held up her hands in surrender. "You got a point. No more wisecracks."

"Thank you."

They started opening drawers and sifting through files. When Vanessa opened a bottom file cabinet she immediately noticed something.

"Bingo," she yelled.

"What you got?" Eric dropped his papers and walked over to her.

"These folders." She pulled several folders from the drawer, laying them on top of the desk. "This is the account that I told you about. Look, the same name—ORICA Services." She opened the file.

"Anything unusual?"

"I can't tell. I'll have to go over everything."

Eric picked up a few folders and walked over to sit

on the couch and leaf through them. The folders were filled with invoices from several different companies, all with Brightline letterhead. All signed by Christopher, or Vanessa.

He looked up at her for a split second, and wondered if she could be looking for evidence to help, or to trash. The next file held a letter-size envelope from Brightline.

"I wonder what he was doing with all these files? Here's copies of some of our transactions, but"—she picked up a stack of invoices, holding them out to Eric—"these aren't ours. Why would he have copies of files from other accounts?"

"Who signed them?" Eric asked as he opened the envelope.

She leafed through the invoices. "Everybody. Jack, Brenda, Mary. Here's a few from people who don't even work there anymore."

Inside the envelope was a sheet of paper. Eric unfolded the paper and read the list of typed names. Christopher's name was number three, Vanessa's was number four.

"Anything over there?" she asked.

He looked up and realized what he had in his hand: "The List." This was the list Vanessa had told him was circulating around Brightline. She was number four.

"No. Just more invoices." He folded the paper and slid it back into the envelope. When Vanessa reached down into the file to pull out more folders, he slid the envelope inside his jacket pocket.

After every piece of paper in the office had been examined to the fullest, Vanessa settled on several files to take with her. "I want to go through these and try to figure out why he had them. What was he on to?"

"Or up to," Eric offered.

Eric walked over to the desk calendar and leafed through the pages. He stopped.

"What you looking for?" she asked.

"The twenty-fourth of April. The page is missing."

"So?"

"That's the day he died."

Twelve

The door popped open slowly, making a creaking sound. He turned and looked over his shoulder. Nothing moved—not a sound, other than the normal residential noises. He didn't see anyone peeping out windows or walking around their yards. In broad daylight he managed to go undetected yet again.

He opened the door wider and stepped inside. The house was quiet and dark. All the shades were pulled closed. He pulled a small flashlight from his back waistband. First, he shone it at his watch. He might not have much time—he didn't know. She hadn't been home all night, but he didn't know when she'd return. He needed to make this fast.

He walked around the kitchen, looking into the refrigerator and through the drawers.

A few minutes later, he started up the stairs that led to the bedrooms.

During the drive back Eric couldn't help but reminisce about the last time he'd gotten involved with someone on a case. Being involved with him had cost Janet her life. His partner warned him not to get involved with a woman who had drug ties. But he didn't listen. Before he knew it, she was spending a night here and there, then days at his house.

The minute he fell in love with her, she was gone. She'd gotten too close to him. Her drug-dealing friends didn't know how much she'd told him, so they'd silenced her. He couldn't let Vanessa get too involved.

"Vanessa."

"Yes."

"When we get back, let me have those files and I'll go through them."

"You don't know what to look for."

"I'll know it when I see it, right?" He glanced over at her.

She shook her head and looked out the window. "No, you probably won't. You don't work with it day in and day out." She raised one eyebrow in a questioning slant. "Why do you want the files?"

"I don't want you involved in this any more than you already are. If there's more to Christopher's death, I don't want to do anything that might get you hurt."

"But I need to prove that he didn't—"

"You don't *need* to prove anything. *He* was charged with theft, not you. Let me work on it. I want you out of it."

"Eric, I gave his sister my word that I would do whatever I could to find something, anything to prove he didn't steal any money. And I intend to keep my word."

"Vanessa, if you get hurt, I—"

"How can I get hurt looking through papers? Oh, I might get a paper cut, but I don't need you to protect me from that."

He sighed. "You are the most stubborn woman I've ever met. I could just take those files from you, you know. It's called evidence."

"I know." She gave him a pleading look. "But you won't. At least not right now. You'll give me a day or two to look through them first, right?"

Eric bit his lip and glanced at her. He was doing it

again. He turned back to the road. What was it about her that made him give in all the damned time? "You've got two days. After that, I'm coming to pick the files up. So you'd better start tonight." He knew he had no right to these files, but she didn't know that.

"Thank you. I'll jump right on it." She reached in the backseat for one of the folders and started leafing through it as they rode.

After stopping for dinner, they pulled up to Vanessa's house after dusk. Eric gave her the keys to the rental car. "Want me to help you up the steps and into the house?" he offered, walking close to her, grinning.

She thought about the kiss the night before and smiled, shaking her head. "That's okay. I'm a big girl you know. Besides, if I need the police, I know how to call."

He backed away, pulled his car keys from his pocket, and pointed at her. "Okay, I get ya. Let me know when your car's ready and I'll drive you back to pick it up. In the meantime, I'll be seeing you in a few days."

"Yeah." She pointed back at him. "And thanks for tagging along."

"You didn't really think I'd let you go alone, did you?"

"Like I said, you didn't seem interested."

"Trust me"—he opened his car door—"I'm interested."

He waited for her to go inside before pulling away. She closed and locked the front door, then peeked out the window. He was gone.

She noticed a late-model green car parked across the street. Something about that car looked familiar. Maybe not, she thought as she dropped the curtain.

Glad to be home and not in that musty little motel room, she needed to shower and get out of those clothes. First, she went into her office and put the folders on her desk. She couldn't believe what a wild weekend it had turned out to be. Betty didn't believe it when she told her she almost lost her life. But she had. If Eric hadn't been driving she might have landed in the draining ditch upside down. It would have killed her for sure.

Halfway up the stairs, the phone rang. She didn't want to answer it. All she wanted to do was take a shower. But it could be her mother wondering if she was coming by for Sunday dinner.

She ran back down the stairs and grabbed the phone. "Hello?" she answered before the answering machine came on.

Sniffles came from the other end.

"Hello," she said again.

"Vanessa, he didn't come home."

It was Betty.

"What are you talking about?"

"We came back last night. Harold went back out the minute we walked in, but never came back." She began to cry. "I don't know what to do. Reggie keeps asking about his father, and I don't know what to tell him." Her sobs grew louder as she talked through them. "He always has breakfast with Reggie on weekends. He's never stayed out all night before. The last time he just didn't show up until about six in the morning."

"Have you called the police?" Vanessa's heart raced. Harold was Betty's world, and she was devoted to him.

"No. I don't know what I'd say."

"Ask them to look for him, Betty. He could have been involved in a car accident or anything. He might be lying on the side of the road somewhere." Now she was getting nervous.

"That's not what's happened to him. I think he's with that witch somewhere." Her sobbing turned into vicious, venomous words. "I'm going to go find him. I know where she lives."

"Betty, don't do that. You don't know if Harold's seeing anyone else or not. What proof do you have?"

"I smell her on him. That's all the proof I need. And dammit, I want my husband back."

Vanessa had never heard Betty this desperate before. Everything in her life had always been so perfect. "Betty, how long have you known about this?"

"Long enough, and today I'm going to do something about it."

"Where's Reggie?"

"He's in his room." She blew her nose and continued sniffling. "That's why I called you. Can you come watch him for me? I'm going to get my husband."

"Betty, don't. Look, I'm on my way. Don't leave the house until I get there."

"Okay, but hurry."

Vanessa slammed the phone down and grabbed the rental car keys and her purse. She wasn't accustomed to Betty needing her like this, but she'd always been there for her. A shower and clean clothes would have to wait.

"I don't understand. I thought things were settled. He committed suicide, didn't he?" John Eagan leaned back in his high-back black leather seat with his arms crossed, looking baffled by Eric's questioning.

"Sir, that's what we're trying to determine. The investigation hasn't been closed yet." Eric sat across the desk from Brightline's president, who seemed to be unaware of the situation his own company was in.

"Hmm." He shook his head. "So how does this *list* you mentioned tie into the investigation?"

"I was told it's some sort of a hit list. I figured if the company has such a list, you would know about it. I mean things like that generate from management, don't they?" Eric never expected him to admit such ownership, but he looked for that slight bit of recognition in his face.

"Not at Brightline they don't. That would be ridiculous. What my staff may have put together was a list of suspected thieves, but a hit list, no way. We're a small computer company; we're not in the business of putting contracts out on people."

Eric reached inside his pocket and pulled out the envelope he found at Christopher's house. Laying it down on the desk, he slid it over to Mr. Eagan.

"Do you have any idea what this is?"

Mr. Eagan looked at the envelope. Eric watched him study the handwriting. It wasn't Christopher's; Eric had already checked into that.

Looking at Eric, Mr. Eagan picked up the envelope and pulled out the paper inside. He carefully studied the contents before speaking.

"These people no longer work with us. Where did you get this?"

"The first three are dead." Eric regarded him skeptically.

"Dead!" He looked down at the list of names again. Was that total surprise on his face, or a good mask?

"The last one still works here. She worked with Christopher Harris, so you can see my concern. If that *is* some type of hit list, she's next."

Visibly shaken, Mr. Eagan folded the paper and reinserted it into the envelope, then laid it next to him.

"I'll have a talk with my management staff, but like I told you, this is probably just a list of suspected thieves. You did say Ms. Benton worked with Christopher Harris, didn't she?"

"Yes, she did."

"Then it's only natural to suspect her involvement in some way if she worked with him."

Eric stood. "I don't believe he ever got a chance to refute the charges."

Mr. Eagan stood also. "Maybe he killed himself because he couldn't."

"If that's the case, then it's my job to prove it." He pointed at the envelope. "I'm sorry. I'll need that back."

Mr. Eagan handed Eric the envelope. "I'm sure, Detective, in your investigation that you'll find Brightline has done nothing wrong. I'm sorry about Mr. Harris, but we can't be blamed for his suicide."

Eric put the list back into his jacket pocket. "Well, sir, let's hope that Ms. Benton doesn't decide to commit suicide. Since it looks like she's next on the list." Eric narrowed his eyes at him. He didn't like this man.

"Yes, let's hope not."

Eric walked out of Brightline not sure if John Eagan was responsible for that list or not. With a little luck, maybe this meeting would shake things up. The death of three suspected thieves in two years sounded like this company was involved. He prayed Vanessa wasn't caught in the middle of something.

Two days later, after speaking with the accountant Eric had going over Brightline's financials, he had an urgent call from a friend.

He suspected it was his anonymous caller again.

"Detective Daniels, are you still handling the Christopher Harris case?"

"Yes, I am." Eric recognized the same muffled voice.

"Did you check out his partner?"

"Do you want to tell me this time who you are?" Anonymous calls annoyed him.

"Was I right?"

"About what?"

"I told you he didn't commit suicide."

"I haven't found any proof of that yet. Do you have any solid proof for me?"

"Who's next on the list, Detective?"

Now the caller had Eric's attention. He sat up in his seat, grabbed a pen, and found a scrap piece of paper. "How's that?"

"I know all about the list. They're about to catch another thief, unless you catch them first."

"Who told you that?" he asked, only to have the dial tone reply. "Hello? Hello?" Nothing.

Eric slammed the phone down in frustration. He should have traced that call. Whoever it was, knew about the list. It had to be someone from Brightline. He pulled the paper from his desk file and examined it again. There was no date. He had no idea when the list was created. For all he knew, Christopher created the list himself.

Combing the company's financial records was taking too long. He needed some fast answers. Looking around his office at the other detectives scurrying about, he had an idea. The secretary. Secretaries knew everything that went on in most companies. If there were any problems at Brightline, she would know. He pulled out a file with personnel information.

Nikki Taylor was a young white female, and a single parent. Perfect, he thought. Now it was time to talk to the communication hub of the company.

Thirteen

Eric pulled into the subdivision off Buford Highway looking for condominium unit 4315. He drove slowly, making sure not to hit any of the numerous children running around the complex. Her unit was near the back. He parked next to her new red Honda Accord. "Nice car," he commented, and made a mental note.

He hadn't called, hoping to catch her off guard. The last thing he needed was some prepared statement the company wanted her to give him. He rang the bell.

Seconds later, the door yanked open and she looked up at him in surprise.

"Hello. Ms. Taylor?"

Her eyes widened and she closed the door a little more. "Yes. What can I do for you?"

"I'm Detective Daniels. Do you remember me?" He held out his badge.

She turned up her lip as she nodded as if to say "So what?" "Yeah, I remember you." She held on to the doorframe.

Her protective stance offered him a challenge. But that was okay; he loved nothing more than a good challenge.

"Ms. Taylor, I was hoping I could talk to you this evening."

"What about?" she fired back at him.

This time Eric chuckled. "Well, the truth of the matter is, I need some information about Brightline. As you know, I'm investigating Mr. Harris's death, and some things I'm hearing don't add up. I just need clarification about a few things."

"Why me?"

"You're the secretary. And who knows more about what's going on at a company than its secretary. I'm hoping you can clear a few misconceptions up for me." He smiled at her, but she still didn't open the door any farther.

"It'll only take a few minutes, I promise." Smiling, he held up his right hand. "I figured it was better if I came to you than to ask you down to the station."

She opened the door wider and glanced up and down the street before inviting him in.

"I'm expecting company so you'll have to make it quick." She stepped aside as he entered.

The inside of the apartment was a different story from the outside. He stepped into the living room, which was laid with a big-screen television, two nice couches facing each other, and some expensive stereo equipment. Next to the patio door were two small bikes.

Eric pointed to the bikes as he sat down. "Your sons'?"

"Yeah." She sat down opposite him on the other couch, crossing her legs and arms. "You know, I told the other police everything I know about Christopher. I don't know how I can help you."

"Actually, I'm more interested in Brightline. How would you say the company's doing right now?"

She shrugged and gave him a blank look. "Okay, I guess. They haven't had to lay off yet like so many other companies are doing."

"So you haven't been asked to curb spending or anything?"

"Well, yeah, but that comes around at least once a

year. Only supplies that are absolutely necessary can be ordered. They limit traveling for a while also.

"But I understand why. You should see the money those people waste. Every week I'm ordering enough office supplies to support a small school. And they refuse to fly with discount carriers."

"Do you think Christopher Harris's theft charges have affected spending, as well?"

She uncrossed her legs. Suddenly she seemed to be searching for something to do with her hands. She tucked a hand underneath her. "I don't know anything about that."

"Mr. Steel never talked to you about it?"

She stood. "You know, I thought you wanted to talk to me about something else. I'm afraid I can't talk about any theft charges."

"You haven't been accused of anything, have you?" he asked, faking a deep concerned expression.

"Of course not." She circled the couch and stood behind it.

He sighed. "That's good. I don't mean to alarm you, but when companies like Brightline have financial troubles they start looking for scapegoats."

She sat on the back of the couch. "Like I said, I'm sorry I can't help you. I don't know anything."

Eric stood and looked over at the bikes. "That's good. The less you know, the better your chances of not being fired."

She laughed. "He won't fire me."

"Sounds like you're pretty sure of that. I guess I was right. You are the lifeline of the company. What would they do without you?"

"Nothing goes on there that I don't know." Realizing what she said, she looked up at him.

He smiled and sat back down. "I understand, but you need to realize how serious this is. Unless you want to be looking for a new job and means to support your sons, I think we need to talk."

"He wouldn't do that," she said, coming back around the couch.

His hunch was right. "Oh, yes, he would. If the company goes down, trust me, everyone goes down with him." For now, Eric wasn't sure what *he* was talking about, but he had an idea. He just needed her to confirm it for him.

"So why don't you tell me what you know about the theft charges and the company's financial position?"

She sank down into her seat and let out a deep sigh.

"Mom, I'd love to talk to you, but I'm running late." Vanessa held the phone between her ear and shoulder, hurrying through the house getting ready for work.

"Dear, I have one more question. What do you think he's up to?"

"Ma, I'm not going to gossip with you about Harold this early in the morning. Call Betty if you want to know what's going on. She'll tell you."

"No, she won't. She's pretending nothing happened." Gladys sounded as if she was pouting.

Vanessa started shoving folders into her tote bag, but a few were missing. "Uh-huh," she said into the phone as she practically turned the desk upside down looking for those folders.

"Are you listening to me?" her mother asked in an annoyed tone.

"Yeah, she's in denial." *Where in the hell are those folders?* She searched the desk again, hoping somehow they would miraculously show up. Nothing.

"What happened between them? What is it she's denying?"

"Mama, you'll have to call Betty and ask her. I don't

have a clue." Okay, so the folders weren't on her desk. She shifted the phone to her other shoulder and scrambled around her office hoping she'd moved the missing files. They weren't on the couch, or on top of the file cabinet.

"Well, since I can't get you to tell me what happened, how's your car?"

"It's still in the shop." She walked through the kitchen, the dining room, even the laundry room. The folders were gone.

"Look, Mom, I've gotta run. I'll see you Sunday, okay?"

"Okay, but before Sunday I want to know what happened, you hear me?"

"Yes, ma'am." Vanessa yanked up her tote bag and ran out the door. She was already thirty minutes late. Ever since Christopher's death, her boss had requested everyone show up on time. They were behind.

All the way to work she searched her brain trying to remember if she'd moved those folders. Did she have them up in her bedroom to go over them? No. She hadn't even looked through the folders yet. Eric was going to kill her. He said she could keep the folders for a few days, then he wanted them. They were evidence, and she'd lost the evidence.

She stepped onto the elevator feeling very uneasy. How could those folders get up and walk away by themselves?

As the elevator door opened, Ronnie started to step on.

"I'm sorry." After he noticed her, he stopped and stood aside, holding the door open.

"Hi, Ronnie. No problem."

"You okay?" he asked, keeping the door open.

She sighed and nodded. "Yeah, I'm fine. Thanks for helping me home that day."

"No problem. How you getting along?" The bell in the elevator rang, so he let the door close.

"Pretty good. How are things going with you?"

"Okay, thingth slowed down a bit. If you need help with thomethin, just let me know. My workload's bearable right now."

"Thanks, Ronnie. You're always so helpful." *And so hard to understand,* she thought. His lisp restricted him from socializing as much as she bet he wanted to.

"Chrithopher wath my friend, too. And I know he had a pretty mean workload. If you need me, juth ask. I might be able to help."

"You know about his accounts?" she asked, curious.

"He talked about them over lunch. I might remember thomething that will prove helpful."

"Did he ever share with you that he was even suspected of stealing money?"

He pressed the button for the elevator again. "No, never. All we ever talked about wath hith workload, and mine. Tho, if I can help, call me."

"Thanks, Ronnie, I'll remember that." Vanessa walked away, curious about how close Christopher and Ronnie really were. Could they have been lovers, too? Ronnie didn't look gay. Then again, neither did Christopher. Were they close enough for Christopher to share his suspicions about the thefts with him? She'd have to find out.

Brenda's terminal was on and a steaming cup of coffee sat on her desk. Vanessa needed to run some ideas by her this morning.

An hour later, Vanessa was heavily into her day when Brenda came back to her desk.

"Vanessa, Jane wants to see you," Brenda said, leaning over the cubicle.

"What's up?" Vanessa asked, getting up.

"Some impromptu review crap. She's calling everybody in one by one to discuss workload and any other bull she can think of. You're up next," she said with a smirk.

Frowning, Vanessa grabbed her empty cup and made a pit stop in the break room. From the look on Brenda's face this wasn't going to be a good meeting.

When she walked in, Jane was on the phone. She motioned for Vanessa to have a seat. Which is what she did. She sipped her coffee and listened to fragmented pieces of Jane's conversation.

She hung up and smiled at Vanessa. "I'm sorry this is on such short notice, but these reviews have to be completed before the end of the week. And since I'm leaving town this afternoon, I need to get you all in today."

Vanessa shook her head. *Okay, so let's get this over with.*

"These reviews are based on the last three months. I know you might not have expected to discuss these issues today, so I'll let you look over them and we can really discuss them when I return." She handed Vanessa her review form.

The first thing Vanessa noticed was the overall rating. Of a possible five score, she had a three, which wasn't very good. "What is this?" There had to be some type of a mistake.

"Well, that's based on workload, and yours isn't quite up to par."

"Excuse me?" Vanessa knew she was handling her own as far as work was concerned. She and Christopher had a full load.

"Well, since the beginning of the year most of the staff has carried a pretty heavy load. How you and Christopher had such a light load I don't know." She paused, looking over the review. "Did you reassign some of your orders over to the team?"

"No, I didn't. I worked every account that was given to me. And we closed out everything on time."

"Yes, I know that, but you did have some delinquent accounts, and there appears to be a miscalculation with your records. Some of the transactions can't be accounted for. Do you know anything about that?"

Vanessa's jaw dropped. "I don't understand. What transactions are you referring to?"

"Offhand I don't know, but Nikki has the files. I'll have her copy them for you. We can't see where payments were made into some account."

Vanessa uncrossed her legs and sat up. "Are you accusing me of losing payments?"

"Oh, no. I'm not accusing you of anything. I'm sure it's all an honest mistake. You may have transposed the account number or something and the money went into another customer's account. We just have to straighten all those situations out. All monies have to be accounted for."

A sinking feeling swept over Vanessa. She knew all her accounts had been processed correctly. She never transposed any numbers, like her boss said.

"And your workload. We'll have to do something about that if you're to improve."

"Improve! I don't understand. Last quarter I was rated a two, and I'm being considered for the promotion in contracts. How can that be possible if I have a three?"

"Yes, well, about that promotion. It hasn't been announced yet, and I trust you'll keep this between us. That position was offered to Mindy. The reason given was that she has a little more time with the company than you. I'm real sorry."

"Mindy in accounting?"

"Mindy Gentry, yes."

"She started a week before I did. That's the blonde with the tight-fitting dresses, right?"

Jane dropped her head and folded her hands together. "Vanessa, I know you're upset."

"You're damn right I'm upset. That's not fair. I thought that position was between Ralph and myself. Where did Mindy come from?"

"She applied for the position, too. But don't worry. Once you get your performance back up, I'm sure—"

"Jane, my performance is fine. I'm sorry, but I disagree with everything in this review." She glanced down at the paper. "Christopher and I worked our accounts like clockwork. I've never come to you for assistance with an account. I've never had a customer complain about anything that I've done. All I do around here is my job, and I do it well."

"I'm sorry. I did everything I could to get you that promotion. We can sit down in a few months to make sure you're on track. In the meantime—" Jane reached over to the edge of her desk and picked up some folders.

Vanessa wanted to throw the review at her and walk out of that office and the building.

"Here are the rest of Christopher's files. I've reassigned them to you. This should bring your workload up to the rest of the team's. All you have to do is prove that you can handle the load with no problems, and we can give you that raise we talked about last time."

Vanessa wanted to explode. She rested her elbow on the chair arm, and pinched her chin between her fingers. They weren't giving her a raise, a promotion, or anything else. She knew it. They'd gotten rid of Christopher; now it was her turn.

"You still want a raise, don't you?" Jane asked.

She was too upset to speak. She needed that raise in order to buy a house. Or she could go out and find a better job. "Of course I still want it. I just don't want to die for it."

Jane cocked her head at Vanessa. "What did you mean by that?"

"I mean, I don't think I'll be around here long enough to take advantage of either. I've made no bones about the fact that I think Christopher was killed, and I think it had something to do with Brightline."

"Vanessa, do you know how ridiculous that sounds?"

"About as ridiculous as Christopher killing himself." She crossed her arms and looked down at the review. There went her new house, and maybe her future at Brightline.

Fourteen

Vanessa stormed back to her desk, bumping people along the way. She threw the folders down, making a loud thumping sound.

Brenda popped up from her seat. "Good meeting, huh?"

"Yeah, we had a blast," she replied sarcastically with her arms crossed. "You know, that woman must have lost her marbles. Suddenly, my rating's dropped and my workload isn't enough."

"I know what you mean. My rating's gone down, too."

Vanessa plopped down into her seat. Wheels were in motion to get rid of her, too, but why? She hadn't stolen any money and they knew that. She hadn't found anything that pointed to anyone, at least that she knew of.

She crossed one arm, and rested her other elbow atop it. "Brenda, something's going on here."

"What do you mean?"

"I don't know exactly. First, they accuse Christopher of theft"—she looked up at Brenda—"which we know he didn't do. Now they're coming after me."

"Who is?"

"Jane. She knows my performance is solid. I'd like to know why she's doing this."

"Don't get so bent out of shape over this. My performance slid from a two to a three, and I know I haven't been doing anything different. Money's tight, so they're trying to weed people out. See who quits under the pressure. You know corporate America."

"Well, there's nothing I can do about it right now. Let's get these orders out of here."

"Yeah, don't worry yourself over it." Brenda sat back down.

Vanessa wasn't sure why Brenda had lied, but she knew Brenda was never a two performer. Something was going on around here and she had to figure out what, before they fired or killed her. She needed to find the list, or whatever evidence she could that Christopher hadn't stolen any money.

As the day moved on, she went to work pulling old records from her computer and printing them. She printed all her old spreadsheets.

As soon as Brenda left for lunch, Vanessa hopped over to Christopher's computer and searched for his old Excel spreadsheets. The company might not give her access to his files, but they'd forgotten about the spreadsheets, which listed all payments made and when. It was going to be a long, drawn-out process, but she could reconcile everything.

She worked till well after quitting time, printing what must have been a ream of paper in spreadsheets. Most of the staff had left for the day by the time she had the courage to pull something out and start looking over it.

Her phone rang.

Why not let voice mail get it since it was after five? But it might be Betty.

"Hello, Vanessa Benton. Can I help you?"

"You sure can. I need to see those files tonight."

Oh, no. It was Eric. "About those files . . ."

"When you weren't at home, I figured you might still be there. Will you be home by eight?"

"I will, but . . ."

"Great. I'll swing by to pick up the folders."

Before she could respond, he hung up.

"Great, I'll go home and search for them," she said, to the receiver. She couldn't imagine what had happened to those folders. "I was in such a hurry this morning, I just missed them," she told herself. Besides, her mother had distracted her.

"Hello, Ms. Benton, working late?"

She turned to see Juan, the janitor, emptying her trash. "Hi, Juan. Yeah, they've got me doing overtime."

"How's that car running?"

"I'm driving a rental right now. I had an accident and the car's in the shop."

"I hope nobody got hurt."

"No. It wasn't that bad. I pick my car up in about a week or so."

"Good. Well, don't you work too late now."

"I was packing it up when you came along."

"Okay, have a nice night now."

"You, too." Ever since her car hadn't started one night and Juan had had to help her, he'd always asked about her car. He was a nice man.

She turned off the computer and left. She wanted to freshen up a bit before Eric arrived. Not like he was coming to see her for social reasons or anything, but a girl had to always look her best. That much she'd learned from Gladys and Betty.

Vanessa hurried home, took a shower, changed into a comfortable sundress, and redid her make-up. She caught her reflection in the mirror and had to back up. "What the hell am I doing?" she asked herself.

His coming here was about Christopher's death. Not her. The man didn't ask her out to the movies, or dinner. It wasn't a date, unfortunately. She stopped primping and went to look for those folders.

At eight o'clock on the nose the doorbell rang. She glanced in the hall mirror before opening the door.

"Hey, there. I'm right on time, aren't I?"

"Yeah. Come on in." She stood back, letting him pass. The woodsy aroma of his cologne came in with him. Instead of a suit, tonight he had on a pair of tan dress slacks and a cool-looking multicolor polo shirt. He looked dressed for a date.

"Try not to sound too happy, will ya."

"I'm sorry, I had a bad day."

"Anything I can do to make it better?" he asked, wearing a wicked grin as she closed the door.

"No, it'll all be over soon, and I can start fresh in the morning."

"So . . . were you able to find anything?" he asked, putting his car keys in his pocket.

"No. And you're not going to believe this."

"What?"

"I can't find the files. I know I laid them in my office when I got home, then my sister called and I had to run out. The next day when I went to work on them, they were gone."

"What do you mean gone? You misplaced them, or they disappeared?"

"I don't know. I remember looking at them and then . . ."

"Where were they?"

"In my office." She gestured toward her office.

They went inside and started looking around. "Have you had any company?"

"No, and I've looked everywhere. They're no longer in the house."

"Is anything else missing?" he asked, walking back to the front door.

"Not that I know of. But I haven't looked. Why?" She crossed her arms.

He walked back into the living room to check the front

door and the front windows. “Files don’t just get up and walk away by themselves.”

“What are you saying?”

“Unless you misplaced them at work, maybe you had a visitor you don’t know about.”

She followed him through the house and into the kitchen.

“Did you tell anybody about the files?” he asked.

“No, not a soul. Are you trying to tell me somebody broke in here and took those files?”

“That’s what I’m saying.” He opened the back door. “Do you always keep your doors locked?”

“Of course.”

He squatted down to examine the lock. “Ever think of investing in a dead bolt, or an alarm system?”

“I’ve never needed one. This is a very safe neighborhood.”

“News flash, Ms. Benton. There’s no such thing anymore. First thing tomorrow, we get you a dead bolt.” He held the doorknob and motioned for her to come look.

“What is it?” A chill ran through her as she walked over to him.

“Don’t touch the door. Somebody jimmied your lock, unless it’s always been like that.”

She squatted down and looked at the lock. “Oh, my God.”

“Who else has a key?”

“Nobody.”

When she stood, Eric closed and locked the door. “I’ll be by early tomorrow. Come on, let’s have a look around.”

Her stomach did a few somersaults. She ran a hand up and down her arm. “You mean after I came in Sunday night, someone broke into my house?”

“Looks like it. I want you to go through everything and tell me what else is missing.”

She combed the house with her heart beating like a drum. The thought that someone had been in her house petrified her. They'd violated her personal space, and could have killed her. The one place she felt safe was now damaged. And for what? A few folders.

"Everything's here. I can't find anything missing," she said when she came down the stairs.

Eric was hanging up the phone.

"Who were you calling?" she asked, curious.

"Somebody who can watch your place for me."

She cleared the landing and walked into her office. "So, what am I going to have—a policeman staked outside my door now?"

"No, but he'll ride through periodically. Do you have a gun?"

"I don't like guns. They kill people. Do you think I need one?" She struggled to control the quivering of her voice.

"I'm wishing you had an alarm system right now. Maybe I should stay here with you tonight." He scratched behind his ear and glanced around her office. His eyes settled on the couch.

"You'd do that?" she asked, surprised.

He returned his gaze to her eyes. "If you're scared of being here alone."

She didn't think she could take another night alone with him. This time she might forget he was a detective and she didn't want to be involved with a detective again. "No, I'll be fine. But thanks for the offer. I have your numbers if I need you."

"Okay." He stood there looking at her.

"So, what are you going to do about the files?"

"I'm going to try and find them. If you remember what accounts they were, write it down for me."

"Sure." She grabbed a piece of paper from her desk

and sat down to make out a list. She'd only brought back four files.

"While you do that, I'm going to have a look around out back."

A few minutes later, Vanessa looked up as Eric walked back into the room.

"Have you talked with Christopher's sister?"

"No, not yet. But I'm supposed to meet her and Sean tomorrow."

"I'd like to talk to him myself. Do you have his number?"

"No, but I can have him call you." She handed him the list.

He looked over the list before folding it and putting it into his pants pocket. "Good." Her stomach made a loud grumbling sound.

Embarrassed, she placed both hands on her stomach and sucked in.

"Hungry?"

"A little, yeah."

"I am, too. Let me take you to a nice place not far from here for a quick bite."

"That's okay. I was going to defrost some chicken."

"My treat. They make the best vegetarian burgers in Atlanta. No peanuts on the floor this time. Sure you won't change your mind?"

On the verge of a migraine headache because she hadn't eaten all evening, her stomach growled again. What the hell—she was dressed, and that chicken wouldn't be thawed for a while. "Okay, let me grab my purse."

After what she'd just found out, being with Eric might be safer than staying home alone. Since that night in Alabama, she'd dreamed of him while she slept and when she was awake. She had erotic steamy dreams that reminded her of the heat during an August backyard barbecue. Sweat-dripping-down-the-crease-of-your-breast type of dreams.

She walked back downstairs and smiled when she saw him standing by the front door waiting for her. He had come by for a date, after all.

The next morning, Eric came by and installed a deadbolt lock, just like he had promised. Vanessa hadn't slept a wink all night. Every time she heard a sound, she peeked out the window. She dressed and went to work early, hoping to get a jump on things before everyone showed up.

The company names she wrote down for Eric she also wrote down for herself. With a huge mug of coffee heavy on hazelnut creamer, she worked at a rapid pace. She searched her archive files for each account. She needed payment histories, E-mails containing the company names, anything that would make her trip to Alabama worthwhile.

Then she noticed something. Neetlebutters Inc. One of the companies on her list was there on the last payment history report. This wasn't one of her or Christopher's accounts. She pulled up the payment transaction and looked at the signature. Jack White.

"That's odd."

From time to time they might have a need to get their boss to sign a payment, but never a peer like Jack. She pulled out the spreadsheet and tried to reconcile the payment amount. After crunching the numbers every which way possible, they still didn't add up. There weren't enough equipment sales to make up the seventy-five-thousand-dollars payments.

"Hey, girl, what you doing here so early?"

Vanessa almost jumped out of her seat. She was so deep into her report she didn't hear anyone come in.

Brenda waved at her as she unlocked her desk. "I scare you?"

"Hell, yeah. I didn't hear you come in." She pulled her papers together and shoved them into a folder.

"Jane's got you humping, doesn't she?"

"What are you talking about?"

"Your review. You said she gave you a lot of extra work."

"Oh . . . yeah. That's why I got in here so early. And I'll probably be working late tonight. I've got so much to do."

"Okay, so lunch is on me. Don't make any plans for today. Us hardworking ladies gotta eat."

"Hey, I'll be ready."

When Brenda went for coffee, Vanessa pulled her spreadsheet back out. She tried to reconcile other payments to make sure everything could be justified. This time she found transactions with no dollar amounts and another payout that didn't add up.

"Need some help with that?"

Startled again, Vanessa looked up. This time Brenda was standing next to her with a cup of coffee in her hand.

"What you doing, reconciling files?"

Damn. She didn't want anyone knowing what she was up to. "Yeah, a few. Jane wants me to make sure these payments are correct."

"Give me some. I can help. I hate to see you working all day and night."

Well, if she didn't tell her what she was up, to, maybe she could help. She grabbed one of Christopher's files although she didn't think anything was wrong with it. "Okay, take this file and this spreadsheet and reconcile it. If you find any discrepancies, just give it to me."

"Will do." She took the files and went back to her desk.

Brenda had always had her back whenever she needed her. Vanessa hoped to be able to repay the favor one day.

Just as she got back into the groove of researching, the phone rang. It was Betty.

"Vanessa, are you busy?"

"No. What's up?" She expected the worst every time Betty called now.

"He's leaving."

"Harold?"

"Yes," she whimpered. "He's leaving me for that bitch."

"Betty, you're not serious." She couldn't believe her ears. Her sister's marriage upon which Vanessa based all marriages, was falling apart.

"Would I joke about something like that?"

Vanessa could tell she'd been crying before she called. "I'm sorry. When's he leaving?"

"Now. Reggie stayed with Mom last night, and they're bringing him home now. Vanessa, I don't think I can take this. What did I ever do to deserve this?" She was getting hysterical and louder.

"Betty, calm down."

"How can I calm down? I'm losing my life. You don't understand. He's taking everything I've worked for and giving it to that little . . ." The phone went silent as if the connection had been dropped.

"Betty, you okay? Betty?"

"No you're not taking that suit I gave you for Valentine's Day."

Arguing and shouting came through the phone. She'd never heard Harold raise his voice before. It sounded serious.

"Betty?" she screamed into the phone.

"You'll take that stuff over my dead body" came faintly through the phone.

That's all Vanessa needed to hear. She slammed the phone down, grabbed her purse, and shot out the door.

By the time she reached Betty's house, Harold was gone and her mother had calmed Betty down.

Harold had packed a small bag and told Betty he needed time to think. Devastated, she'd thrown a fit. Gladys was in the kitchen preparing Reggie's lunch, while her husband, Otis, sat in the den. Reggie was playing with his cars in the middle of the floor.

"I can't believe this is happening to her," Vanessa said, sitting at the kitchen table drinking a glass of water.

"Neither can she. Her life revolves around that man. You know, she's not like you."

"What do you mean by that?"

"You've got your job to keep you busy. You're just like your father. All work, all the time. No time left for romance, or a family. Besides, you don't need a man."

"Who said I didn't need a man?"

"You did, remember?" Gladys gave her daughter a raised-brow grin.

"Yeah, well, that was a long time ago. Come on, no matter what I say, every woman wants what you and Betty have. Work can't take the place of a man."

"But you seem to be getting along fine. Are you dating anyone?"

"No. I don't have the time right now anyway. I'm helping the police find out who killed Christopher."

Gladys set Reggie's sandwich down and turned to her daughter. "What do you mean you're *helping* the police? Don't do nothing foolish now."

"It's nothing, Mama. I'm just helping Detective Daniels find some things to prove it wasn't suicide."

"Vanessa, I don't like the sound of that. You need to let the police do that themselves. Did he ask for your help?"

"Not exactly, but if I don't help, I might lose my job."

"Would this be the same detective you spent the night with last weekend?" Gladys went back to completing Reggie's lunch.

"Man, Betty's got a big mouth. But it wasn't like that."

"I certainly hope not. I hate to see you make the same mistake twice. I should hope you learned something."

"Mama, Detective Daniels is nothing like Tony. He's really a nice man. Besides, I'm not interested in him anyway."

"Yeah." Gladys glanced back at her daughter. She picked up the tray with Reggie's food on it. "Uh-huh, I hear you talking. Keep on telling yourself that."

Fifteen

"I don't think this is right. Don't you have enough?"

"What constitutes enough? How about what they've done to you? Are you satisfied with what you have?"

"No, but do you have to kill her? There has to be another way."

"There's no other way. You know what you have to do."

"I know. I don't like it, but I know."

"Good." He rubbed his palms together.

"Did you get rid of those files?"

"I'm taking care of everything I'm supposed to. You handle that cop. I don't like him snooping around."

"What am I supposed to do about him?"

A soft knock at the door caught their attention. "Excuse me, sir."

They turned around, surprised that the door wasn't closed.

"Yes, Nikki, what do you want?"

"Sir, Mr. Turner wanted me to run the weekly accounting report right up to you." She walked in and handed him the report while glancing down at the folders on his desk.

"Thank you, Nikki." He dropped the report on top of the files.

She gave his guest a curt smile and walked out.

"Oh, Nikki," he called as she stepped out.

She stopped and turned around. "Yes."

"Close the door behind you, please."

"Yes, sir." She pulled the door to, giving it a slight slam.

They turned to each other. "Is she going to be a problem?" she asked with raised brows.

"No. None whatsoever. I've got that under control."

"Let's hope so."

"I'm sorry I don't have better news. Have you spoken to the police?" Vanessa asked Sean, sitting in Gina's den.

"No. An officer called the house, but I was out of town. I don't know how they got my number."

"I'm afraid I might be to blame for that. You see, Detective Daniels went with me to Alabama. I kind of had to tell him about you. He wanted to know how come I had a key."

"That's okay. I should probably talk to them anyway. I was hoping you'd find something to solve everything. But if you had, I would have surely had to have a conversation with the police then."

She handed over the key. "Well, I did find something. It's just that it's missing now. I never even had a chance to go over what was in the files, before someone broke in and stole them from my house."

"You're kidding!" Sean rose to the edge of the seat, eyeing her. "Do you know who it was?"

"No. But I know it has to do with Brightline. Only they would be interested in those files."

"Man, I'm surprised someone didn't find out about Alabama and break in there."

"That's a very nice place you have there—very upscale. Did you use a decorator?"

"Yes, I hired a firm from Montgomery. They did a great job."

"I bet it wasn't cheap."

Sean looked at Vanessa, then quickly turned away. "Actually, it was quite reasonable. Most of the accessories I've collected over the years." He turned back to her. "I travel quite a bit. Last year, Chris and I went to Italy. We brought back quite a few treasures."

Vanessa didn't like playing around with him. "Sean, what I really need to know is how could Christopher afford a place that big on his salary? It looked pretty funny to the detective, since the day before he was found dead, Christopher was accused of stealing."

Sean straightened his back and narrowed his eyes at her. "So you think he stole money to furnish the house?"

"I don't, but the police might wonder."

"Just about everything in that house is mine, bought and paid for. And I've got the receipts if anyone wants to see them. The antiques were inherited from my grandmother. She was a very wealthy woman. Chris lived with me!"

She smiled. "I knew there was a good explanation."

"I suppose I need to call the police and clear up any misunderstandings that I can. And I want all of that Brightline stuff out of my house. I don't want someone breaking in there. Aren't you scared?"

She shrugged. "Not anymore. Whatever I had—they've got now."

"So you never did find out what he was on to?"

"Not yet, but I haven't stopped trying."

"Vanessa, be very careful. I'm convinced Chris knew who really stole that money. And I think they found out he knew."

"Eric, the chief wants to talk to you. It's about that Alabama trip. He asked me how you did." Harper threw a wad of paper at Eric.

"What did you tell him?" Eric looked up and caught the paper.

"I told him he'd better talk to you."

"Thanks." He threw the wad back across his desk.

When Eric walked in, Torello was on the phone. Eric walked over and sat across from his desk. The bookcase behind him was filled with law books and police procedural manuals. Eric admired his boss. He was a fair man. However, those around him weren't quite as fair.

"Yeah, don't waste another minute on it. He's here now. Call me when you've got something." Torello hung up and stood.

"Daniels, I've got a case I need you on. How's that suicide case going?"

"Sir, I'm not sure that it was suicide."

He started around his desk, but stopped and looked at Eric. "Got any solid proof?"

"No, sir, not yet. But we ran a second autopsy and found some head trauma. We're running a trace on the gun also. I think—"

"Put it on the back burner. Something else has come up." He continued around the desk to a credenza by the window. "I want you and Harper to work this one together."

Eric stood. "But sir, I believe this is a homicide case, not a suicide. It looks like something's going on at Brightline. I'm having the company checked out. It's all in my report."

"But as the primary, you don't have any hard evidence right now, do you?" Torello held up his hands.

Eric looked him dead in the eye, not wanting to admit he didn't have anything solid yet. All he had was a gut feeling and some phony accounts that he hadn't traced to anyone yet. He finally looked away.

"That's what I thought. Detective, if you want my job someday, close that case and move on to something else.

You can get back to it later." He picked up a manila folder from the credenza.

"If I want your job, proving Christopher Harris was murdered is a step in the right direction."

Torello stood holding the folder and studying Eric.

"I'll never get your job if I can't handle this case. Let me prove it, sir. I know I can." Eric could see the apprehension in his boss's eyes.

"Daniels, I like you." He carried the folder back to his desk and sat down. "You've got two weeks." He pointed at Eric. "Bring me something solid in two weeks, or close the case." He looked down at the folder on his desk. "I'll assign someone else to start the interviewing, for a week or so, I guess." He cut his eyes at Eric.

"Thanks, sir." He stood to leave.

"I mean it. You hear me? Two weeks. Now, tell Powell to get in here."

Eric went back to his desk and pulled out everything he had on the case. Then he called Harper over. They'd already begun researching the backgrounds of all the names on the list. Now he had to beef things up.

Two weeks. That was all he had to prove Christopher Harris had been murdered, and the same thing was about to happen to Vanessa, unless he could stop it.

Vanessa turned on the small clock radio she kept in the kitchen. Whenever she was in the mood for cooking, she liked to sing while she cooked.

She'd gotten out a piece of paper and wrote down everything she'd discovered that might help with proving Christopher's innocence. As she cooked, she tried to place all the pieces together. So far she had: the strange payments with Jack's name on them, the disappearing files, the phony companies, the list, a lot of nothing. *Somehow this stuff has to be connected.* If the list actually existed, she needed to get her hands on it. Maybe it would hold the clue.

The doorbell rang.

"Now, who could that be?" She wiped her hands and hoped Betty wasn't at the door. Right now she was in a good mood and didn't want to be brought down.

She swayed her hips and snapped her fingers to "Smooth Operator" as she listened to Sade on the radio. She peeked out the window. Eric stood with his back to her, and his hands crossed behind him.

He spun around as the door opened. A seductive smile crept onto his face as he took her in. Was she naked or something? He seemed to be devouring her as he licked his lips.

"Detective, what can I do for you?" she asked with a flip of her hair. She eyed him from head to toe. Could he possibly look even better tonight than he had any other time? However, he did look tired and in need of a massage.

He popped his lips and stepped closer to the door. "Do you really want to know the answer to that question?" He lowered his head and gazed at her as if she were his favorite lemon meringue pie.

Vanessa twisted her lip into an almost frown to keep from blushing. "Are you flirting with me?" she asked, a coy smile on her face.

"You might say that. Or, then again, you might say I was referring to the case."

"Oh, come on in. I guess you're here on official business." She held the door open and he walked in past her. She closed it behind him.

"I hope it's not a bad time, but I did need some information." Information he knew he could have gotten over the phone.

She walked past him. "Come on in. I'm cooking."

He followed her into the kitchen. "That's what I like—

a woman who loves to cook. Having garden burgers again?"

"No, but I know you didn't drop by for one."

"Most definitely not. My boss wants me to close the case." He hated to drop it on her like that, but there was no smooth way.

"What?" She stopped and spun around. "You can't."

Eric shrugged. "I've got two weeks to come up with something solid." He walked over to the small round kitchen table and sat down.

Vanessa turned the radio down and turned over her turkey cutlets, before going over to the table to join him. "This is crazy. You can't close the case. I know Christopher was murdered. What about the gun? It wasn't his. Did you find out yet who it belongs to?"

He shook his head. "It was reported stolen last year. My partner's working to trace it. What about his boyfriend? I can't get in touch with him. Have you talked to him?"

"Yeah, he's been out of town. I don't think he knows anything, though."

"Why hasn't he spoken to the police?"

She shrugged. "Don't know."

He looked down and noticed the piece of paper Vanessa had been writing on. "What's this?" He picked it up.

"Oh." She reached across the table, looking at the paper. "I was jotting down the things I've found so far. Since seeing Sean, I've been thinking about Christopher." He read her list aloud, stopping when he got to, "the list." "What's this last thing?"

"Remember, I told you his sister said something about a list going around? I've got to find out if that list exists."

"No, you don't." He dropped the paper back on the table. His expression and mood changed.

She got up to check her food. "Why not?" she asked with her back to him.

"Because. I asked you to stay out of this. I just need to get in touch with Christopher's boyfriend."

"His name is Sean."

"Yeah, that's what I meant—Sean." He stood and walked over to the stove and stood next to her. "But I want you to let me take care of everything. Don't get yourself any more involved than you already are. If you happen across anything, or remember anything, call me, page me, or come see me. I just don't want you doing anything to get yourself hurt."

She looked up into his eyes, and for a moment, forgot he was a detective. He was merely a handsome man, trying to protect her. She felt safe with him there. The sound of his voice relaxed her body, even when he sounded excited, like now.

"Promise me you'll do that?" He stood there, not taking his eyes from her until she answered him.

"Okay, I promise." She put the lid down on the skillet.

He sniffed. "Mmm, something smells good."

"Hungry?"

"Is that an invitation?"

"Consider yourself invited. If you like turkey cutlets, then prepare yourself for a treat."

"And to think you didn't even know I was coming by."

She crossed her arms and looked up as he winked at her. She pointed toward the hall bathroom. "Go wash your hands. I'll set the table."

Vanessa fixed him a plate and they spent the next hour eating, drinking, and talking. Never in a million years did she think she'd be sitting down with a policeman again and enjoying herself. Eric was so easy to talk to. He listened to her when she talked, and seemed so interested in whatever she had to say.

After an hour and a half, he had to leave. She walked him to the front door.

He lingered in the doorway before leaving. "Thank you for the dinner. It was great."

"You're welcome."

"Vanessa, can I talk to you about something personal?"

"Sure. As long as it's not too personal." She laughed.

"I don't want you snooping around at work. But if you just have to talk to somebody, you can talk to me. Not because I'm the detective on the case, but because you want to talk to someone."

"Thanks, Eric."

"I mean it. Things are going to heat up. And you might run into something before I do. If that happens, let's talk about it. I want to be here for you. Hell, even if it's not about the case, I don't mind."

She shook her head, not sure what to say. She had feelings for Eric that she couldn't squash. Every day she tried not to think of him, but she always did.

"Eric, that wasn't personal at all. And, yes, I will call you if I need to talk."

"Well, I don't know if you have a man. I mean, you haven't mentioned anyone, or anything. So I just want you to know it's cool to call . . . if you need to . . . for anything."

She couldn't stop smiling. "No, I don't have a man in my life right now. How about you? Will somebody else answer the phone?"

"No, call anytime. I'm available to you twenty-four hours a day."

"Thanks."

"Seven days a week."

They burst into laughter.

"I better get out of here before you have me confessing my sins. Lock the door, and take care." He shook his head and walked down the steps, still smiling.

She smiled and kept laughing. *My, my, the detective is sweet on me.* She closed the door.

"Hey, girl, here's that file you gave me to reconcile." Brenda reached over the wall to hand Vanessa a folder.

"Did it reconcile?"

"Not quite. It's off a little. What did you guys do?"

Vanessa pulled the folder from Brenda's hand, not meaning to snatch it. "How much is a little?" She flipped through the pages.

"I've made note on the last page. A little over fifteen thousand." She pointed when Vanessa reached the last page. "There, at the bottom."

Vanessa glanced up at her before reading the figure. "How could this be?"

"It's probably just an oversight. You probably forgot to record one of the deposits. I wouldn't worry about it."

"Brenda, I have to worry about it. I need to figure out what happened to this money before somebody decides I stole it." She pulled her bottom drawer open and pulled out two more files.

"You don't think they'll do that, do you? What's that?"

"Nothing."

"Excuse me." A high-pitched male voice came from behind Brenda.

She turned and Vanessa looked up. "Are you Vanessa Benton?"

"No, she is." She pointed at Vanessa.

He walked past her to Vanessa's cube. "Sorry. Hi, I'm Matt. I need to remap Christopher Harris's computer. I was told to find you, and I'd find the computer."

"Yeah, it's over there." Vanessa pointed at Christopher's desk and computer still sitting across from her.

"Thanks." Matt took Christopher's seat and turned on his computer.

The young computer geek went to work, giving her an idea. She hadn't been able to get into all of Christopher's files. They were password protected. Maybe Matt could help with that.

She fiddled around with her work until Brenda left for a meeting. Matt was still hard at work. Vanessa got up and walked over to Matt. "How's it going?"

"Fine. It'll take a little bit."

"What will they do with the computer?"

"Get it ready for somebody else."

"How about his files?"

"I'm gonna wipe them out."

"Matt, can you open password-protected files?"

"Yeah, but I'm not supposed to." He gave her a crooked grin.

"But you're gonna wipe them out anyway, right?"

He gave an apprehensive nod. "Well, yes. Is there one you wanna look at?" His fingers kept flying over the keys.

Vanessa pulled up a chair and sat next to him. "Can you open his Word files?"

"Yeah, just a minute." He keyed in a few more things, before jumping to Word. "Which one?"

Vanessa looked at the file names, not sure which one to check out. She wanted to look at them all. "I'm not quite sure." Then she saw a file named Ringo. Christopher had loved his dog. "Can you open that one?" She pointed to the file.

"Done." After a few keystrokes the file opened.

"Great. Can I look at that?" She motioned for him to get up.

"Yeah, I'm gonna run and get a Coke. I'll be right back." He left her to look over the file.

Vanessa scanned through the file. The first page read like a memo to file. On the second page, Christopher listed all his accounts and every transaction processed against them. Page three was labeled Research.

There it was. Unaccounted-for transactions. Dates, amounts, approvals, everything she could imagine. ORICA, Neetlebutters, just what she needed. And it was still on his computer! She couldn't believe it. She hit the print button.

While the document printed, she dashed over to her desk and pulled out a diskette. She could hear Matt talking to someone at the end of the aisle. She threw the diskette in and copied the file. She pulled out the diskette and wrote Ringo on the label.

"All finished?" Matt returned with a Coke in hand.

She jumped and slid the diskette off the desk and into her pocket. "Yep." She closed the file.

She got up and Matt took the seat. "Okay, I'll just finish this up."

"Thanks, Matt. I really appreciate that." She patted him on the back and headed for the printer.

Sixteen

Painstakingly, Vanessa sat on the floor of her home office with papers scattered everywhere. With the precision of a surgeon she went over each account. Christopher had given her a good start. His report outlined transactions, and payouts that were signed by someone other than himself.

Like Sean said, Christopher had found something. He'd made a record of most of it. So far, it totaled just over fifty thousand dollars.

"My God" was all she could say. She sat back against the couch and looked at the papers. These had to be the transactions they had accused him of embezzling. But how was he supposed to have gotten that money? Eric checked his personal accounts, and it wasn't there. If Christopher had stolen that money, he could have been sent to prison.

If he didn't take the money, where did it go? Pulling her knees up close to her chest, she sat in that position thinking for a few minutes. Okay, he was aware money was missing, but how long did he know before they approached him? It had to have taken him some time to pull all these records together. Why hadn't he mentioned any of this to her? A slight chill ran through her. She got up to turn down the air conditioner and went into the kitchen.

She filled the teakettle with fresh water and turned on

the stove. Christopher was a very private person. He didn't talk to her about his troubles at work, or about his personal life. And still, they worked together like a well-oiled machine. Occasionally, he would mention going on a date or two, so she knew he dated women from time to time. Or she thought he had. Since meeting Sean, she wondered if it was all a lie. And if he could lie about that, what else had he lied about?

Why was she so positive he hadn't stolen the money? If he didn't trust her with knowing he was gay, he could have kept anything from her. Maybe he did take the money.

She walked back into the office waiting for her water to boil. If he had taken that money, how had he gotten the transaction to go through without her signing it also? She signed every transaction of his, like he signed every one of hers. All of them had to have two signatures before accounting would process. And what about the payments made without her knowledge? Maybe he got Jack to sign them for him? Maybe they were in it together? But what about the ones with her signature? Who forged those?

She went back into the kitchen to fix a cup of coffee. Before she took a sip, she reached in the drawer for some pain pills. A headache was coming on.

Eric walked around the outside of Dugan's Sports Bar just after dusk, checking out the crime scene again. Maybe Christopher had left a clue that was overlooked. He couldn't believe that no one saw anything until five o'clock in the morning when the body was discovered. Several people had seen him in the club, and agreed that he left alone. However, no one remembered the time.

His car had been parked a block from the club's entrance. But to get a parking spot that close to the club, he had to get there early or get lucky.

Eric looked around at the businesses located within the block. Only the twenty-four-hour Waffle House across the street had been open when the body was found. He had already read over all those interviews and as usual, nobody saw anything. Time to get his own interviews. He crossed the street.

The restaurant was busy as usual, but once he flashed his badge he didn't have a problem getting the waitress to talk to him.

"Yeah, I was on duty that night. When the club closes, those kids usually pack the place, you know. I already told the cops all this." She pushed up the back of her upswept blond ponytail that was slowly coming undone.

"I realize you've already been interviewed. I'm just following up in case you remember anything about that night that you may not have initially told the police officers."

She shook her head and smiled nonchalantly, then gave him a blank look. "Nothing unusual about that night. Just a bunch of rowdy young people, like every Friday night. Sorry, Detective."

"Okay, well, if you do remember something"—he pulled out a business card and handed it to her—"give me a call. Anytime, day or night."

She glanced at the card before shoving it into her uniform pocket. Eager to get back to work, she replied, "Sure will."

Outside, Eric saw a young man dumping the restaurant's garbage. "What the hell." He walked over and decided to ask a few questions.

"Excuse me, can I talk to you a minute?" Eric flashed his badge at the same time he stopped him.

The young man lifted his baseball cap and scratched

the side of his head as he squinted at the badge. "Yeah, what I do?"

Eric chuckled. "I'm talking to people about the guy who was found dead in his car across the street a couple of weeks ago."

"Yeah, man, I was here when they found him. Saw all those police cars swarming around the place."

"Did you see him before the police showed up?"

The young man looked back at the restaurant before answering. "Yeah, I saw him."

A rush of adrenaline ran through Eric's body. He reached into his jacket pocket and pulled out a small pad and pencil. "Can you tell me what you saw?"

"Yeah." The young man used his hands to gesture as he talked. "I was outside smoking a square, when I saw your boy—the dead guy—come out over there and walk up to another dude. I remember them because they were dressed better than most of the folks going in that joint. They got in this old green car and drove off. Your boy left his car down from the club."

"What time was this?"

"Around ten-thirty. That's when I usually step out for a smoke."

"And you saw both men from over here?"

"Yeah, that joint's lit up like a Christmas tree. The one they say committed suicide walked out and stood around for a while. Then the other guy pulled up and got out of the car. He left it double-parked in the street. I thought the cops was gonna pull around the corner and give him a ticket, but they didn't. Cops are pretty hot on parking violations around here. Then they got in the car and took off."

Eric was writing frantically. "Did you see them return?"

"Naw, man, I was back inside working. But I'll tell you this much. At first he didn't look like he was getting in the car. He started to walk off. I looked away a second. When I looked back he was getting inside. After he got in, the driver looked up and down the street before getting in. Like he was looking for somebody or something. It looked a little suspicious to me."

"And you remember all that?"

"Yeah, like I said, them dudes weren't dressed like the typical laid-back crowd of that place. They were kind of older, you know."

"What's your name?"

"Wade, Wade Holmes." He looked over as Eric wrote his name down.

"Did you give a statement to the police already?" Eric asked with a frown. He would have seen this statement for sure.

"No." He shrugged and gave Eric a cocky smile. "I left a little after all the cops showed up. I get off at six. Then I got locked up the next day. Just got out a couple days ago."

"What for?"

He dug his hands deep into his pockets. "Child support."

Wade didn't look more then twenty years old, Eric thought. "Do you think you can give me a description of the guy in the green car?"

"I can try."

"Great."

The next morning, armed with a little more information, and pumped that he was about the crack this case, Eric went to visit Sean, Christopher's lover. Could he have been the man in the old green car? His lover was killed and he hadn't spoken to the police. Sounded funny to him.

Sean gave him an address in midtown. Eric was familiar with the swanky shops and upscale restaurant area. He also knew the area to be a large gay community. He found the architecture firm located in a small renovated house.

Sean ushered him into his office and closed the door behind him. Right away, Eric didn't like the way Sean appeared to be rushing.

"Have a seat, Detective. I have a few minutes before I need to leave. What would you like to know?"

"Thank you, Mr. Gardner, I appreciate you talking with me."

"Call me Sean."

"Okay, Sean. What was your relationship to Christopher Harris?"

Sean stared at him. "We were partners . . . and lovers."

He'd hesitated, as if he wasn't about to mention they were lovers. Eric wondered why. Surely he was aware that Eric knew.

"When was the last time you saw him?"

"Friday morning, before he left for work."

"You didn't see him after work?"

"No, he never came home after work."

"Was that unusual?"

Sean shrugged. "Not really. He sometimes went out after work. But he was usually home by nine or ten. I called several times during the evening, but he never answered. Around eight o'clock, I left for the airport. I was in Virginia on business until Gina reached me Saturday evening."

"Did he say anything about meeting somebody that day?"

"No. He got up and got dressed as usual and went to work. If I hadn't been leaving town that night we would have been in Alabama that weekend."

Eric made a mental note to make sure his trip checked out.

"Do you live with Mr. Harris here in Atlanta?" Eric didn't remember anything in the file about Christopher having a roommate, yet Sean had been there with him Friday morning.

"No. Periodically we crashed at each other's places. I stayed there on Thursday night, because I was leaving town on Friday. I knew I wouldn't see him for a couple of days."

"How often did you guys stay in Alabama?"

Sean looked at his watch, uncrossed and recrossed his legs. "Just on weekends."

"What is it, some sort of a getaway? A retreat from the busy city?"

Sean smiled. "You could say that. Luverne is a small quaint town, much slower than Atlanta. Peaceful. We had planned to relocate and start our own business. I'm not sure what I'll do now."

"Mr. Gardner, after all the interviews, not one person mentioned your name, or that Mr. Harris was gay. How long had you known him?" Eric noticed that question made Sean uncomfortable, but not as uncomfortable as it made him. His approach probably left a lot to be desired.

"We've been friends for over three years. I purchased the house in Alabama a couple of months ago. Chris was coming to live with me."

Sean's face showed signs of stress. For the first time, Eric noticed the more he talked, the sadder he looked.

"I know how you feel about your friend's death, but I have to ask you a few more questions. Was he depressed about anything? Was everything okay between you two?"

"Christopher was never depressed. He complained a lot, but that was just his way. And we got along perfectly.

He was sharper than they'd counted on. That's what it was. You know, he majored in math. I bet they didn't know that."

"Did he ever mention to you what was going on at Brightline?"

Sean tilted his head and shrugged. "From time to time he might have mentioned something—nothing that I can remember, though. That's why I gave Vanessa the key, hoping she could look over things and figure out what he'd stumbled on to. He'd been going over files for weeks. He found something, but I don't know what it was."

"Ms. Benton and I found some files at your Alabama home that Christopher had taken from work."

Sean sat up straight in his seat and cleared his throat. "He didn't steal any money, that's for sure. And I believe he knew someone was coming after him, so he was trying to prove his innocence. They were trying to put him in a trick bag."

"Who's they?"

"Some fools at Brightline. Christopher had no reason to steal any money from that place. The amount they say he's stolen—he's got twice that much in investments. If he was going to steal some money, don't you think he'd steal more than he's got?"

Now it was Eric's turn to shrug. "That's not for me to say. My job is to find out if he committed suicide, or was murdered."

Sean looked at his watch. "I'm sorry, Detective. I've got a meeting that I'm already late for."

"Sure." Eric stood, looking around Sean's high-tech office as he pulled out a business card.

"Well, Mr. Gardner, if you think of anything else, give me a call."

Sean set the card on his desk.

"I was just wondering something."

"Yeah?" Sean asked, picking up his organizer and locking his desk.

"I'm a little curious as to why you didn't come down to the station and give a statement."

Sean shrugged. "No one asked me." He walked out from behind his desk and to the doorway with Eric. "Besides, I hate police stations, and I've got a few pesky parking tickets that I thought might come up."

Eric couldn't believe what had just come out of his mouth. His lover dies and he's scared of a few parking tickets? No way. Something about this guy wasn't right.

The next morning, Vanessa dressed and left for work so fast, she used her fingers as a comb once in the car. She couldn't wait to get to work and meet with Jane. She'd figured out who the thief was, and it wasn't pretty.

She dropped her tote bag on her desk and decided to skip the coffee. She was hyper enough this morning.

"What's up, girl? Why you banging things around over there?" Brenda leaned over the cube, smiling at Vanessa.

"I'm just pulling some things together before I go talk to Jane. I found it."

"Found what?"

"The discrepancies." She shoved everything into a large gold envelope. "I can't talk about it right now, but I'll tell you after I talk with Jane. And you aren't going to believe what's going on around here."

"No kidding! What did you find?"

"Can't talk now, gotta run." She grabbed up her envelope and marched off to Jane's office. On the way she walked past Jack's cube. Lucky for him, he wasn't there.

Jane was on the phone when Vanessa walked in, but Vanessa wasn't leaving. She took a seat and set the gold envelope on Jane's desk. Jane looked down at the folder, then back up.

Vanessa smiled and crossed her arms. She knew she had something, and she wanted Jane to know.

"Mitch, I'll have to call you back. One of my employees needs me right now." Jane hung up the phone. She let out a sigh as she looked down at the envelope again. "What is this?"

"Proof" was all Vanessa said.

Jane picked up the envelope. "Proof of what?"

"That Christopher was set up and it hasn't stopped. Now he's trying to set me up."

Jane peered at her as she opened the envelope. She slid the papers out onto the desk and examined them. Without saying a word she read over Vanessa's attached note first.

Vanessa had summarized all her finds into a note and attached the paperwork as backup. She uncrossed her arms and watched Jane's facial expression as she read over the note. Once or twice Jane looked up at her, but kept reading.

Everything was there, Vanessa thought—the deposits that Jack had signed, and the ones with her forged signature on them. She could only assume that Jack had forged her signature. He was the thief, not Christopher.

After Jane read everything, she leaned forward to rest on her forearms. "Vanessa, you are aware that the Neetlebutters account was a very special account?"

"No, I wasn't."

"That's not unusual. Since Christopher was the senior between the two of you, he probably handled that account himself. This one was set up outside the system. The company would have lost some five hundred thousand dollars' worth of business, had we not rushed this account through."

"What about the other accounts? I didn't sign those checks."

Jane picked up the paper. "Maybe you just don't remember signing them."

"No, I remember every account I sign off on. And I didn't sign any of those. You said something to me before about money missing. There it is." She pointed at the papers.

"Let me keep these and I'll look into it." Jane picked up all the papers and slid them back into the envelope.

Those papers were all the proof Vanessa had. She'd stormed into Jane's office so fast, she hadn't made herself a copy. Hopefully, she wouldn't need one.

"Vanessa, you're a good worker, and Brightline doesn't want to lose you. So don't think anyone's out to get you. If somebody's been tampering with the payments, I'll find out about it. But if I find out you were working with Christopher, I'm going to have to let you go."

"Jane, he didn't steal anything. Look over what I gave you. I think the money Christopher is accused of taking is all right there, with Jack's signature on most of the sign-offs. And I can't believe Christopher was aware of that. If anybody would sign off for him it would be me, not Jack."

Jane stood. "Like I said, Vanessa, let me look into it. I'll get back to you."

"Yeah, okay, but don't lose anything. That's my only copy." She stood and headed for the door.

"And, Vanessa."

She stopped in the doorway and turned around. "Yes."

"Just for the record, I don't believe Christopher stole anything, either."

"Thanks, Jane." Vanessa left Jane's office assured her boss would help her get to the bottom of everything. Maybe her job wouldn't be in jeopardy if the company launched an investigation.

Vanessa hadn't wanted to take a chance on word getting to Jack and have him trying to steal what little evidence she had left, so she collected everything in an envelope and caught the elevator down to the parking desk and threw the envelope into the trunk of her car. She wanted to tell Brenda what'd happened, but she wasn't at her desk.

On her way back into the building she spotted an old green car parked in its usual spot in the back of the garage. She knew she'd seen that car before.

She looked around to see if anyone was in the garage, and she didn't see a soul. She needed a closer look. Jiggling her keys in one hand, she walked over for a closer look. The old Oldsmobile looked to be on its last legs. A huge cross with rhinestone studs hung in the rearview mirror.

"Not leaving, are you?" came a loud voice across the garage.

Vanessa jumped and stepped back from the car. She looked around to see if anyone was talking to her. She saw James from accounting headed toward her.

"You leaving already?" He smiled as he approached.

Was that his car? "No, I just came down to put something in my car."

"Is that yours?" he asked, pointing at the Oldsmobile.

"No, I was just about to ask you the same thing."

He shook his head and hit the alarm on the car parked two cars down from the Oldsmobile. "No, it might be Jack's, though. I saw him coming from back this way one time. Whoever's it is, it's time for a paint job, wouldn't you say?"

"Yeah." She laughed as she moved away from the car. "My dad had one like it years ago." She had to come up with something to explain why she was snooping around someone's car.

"Well, gotta run to the dentist. Catch you later."

"Bye, James." She went back upstairs, sure that same

car had been parked across from her house. Jack was watching her for some reason. And if he was at his desk, she'd find out why.

Seventeen

Brenda tried all afternoon to get out of Vanessa what had happened in Jane's office. However, Vanessa had decided it was best to wait until there was really something to talk about.

She didn't know if Eric had come up with anything else or not, but he'd probably be glad to know that she had. Then again, she thought, he might not be. He hadn't wanted her snooping around, as he put it, anymore.

On the way home, she stopped at the grocery store. She was in a cooking mood again tonight. When she got home, she pulled around to the back to take the groceries in. From her spot on the driveway she could see her back deck. Two potted plants had fallen off the step and lay in pieces on the ground. Had they fallen, or been knocked over by someone? She only used her cell phone in emergencies, and a possible break-in constituted an emergency. She reached into her purse and pulled out her phone and wallet. Quickly, she dialed Eric and he told her to sit tight until he got there.

Again, he got there so fast, she wondered how far away he'd been. He pulled into the driveway behind her car.

"You didn't go inside, did you?" he asked, frowning as he approached her car.

"No. I know better than that. Why do you think I called you?" She talked to him from the rolled-down window. Her motor was still running and the air conditioner was on.

"With you, that doesn't mean a thing. Give me the key and stay right here." He took the key from her, opened the back door, and went inside.

She sat in the car looking all around the house. If someone ran from the house, she wanted to be able to see them. Not that she could do anything. A few minutes later, Eric walked out of the house and motioned her in.

With grocery bags in hand she slowly walked into the house. "Are you sure everything's okay?"

"Yeah, it was probably a cat or a possum. Let me help you." He reached out and took the bags from her.

She ran back out to the car and brought in the envelope that held what little proof she had left. She went straight into her office with it.

"What's that?" Eric asked, following her into the office and pointing at the Brightline envelope he recognized. "Bringing work home with you?" he asked when she put it on the desk.

"No." She went back into the kitchen to put away her meat. "It's what proof I have left that Christopher was not a thief."

"It's what?" His eyebrows came together in a frown.

"Eric, I know what you said, but I think I cracked it. I found those missing deposits, and Jack signed a few, but the others had my signature forged on them." She began putting her groceries away.

"So what did you come up with?" he asked, standing in the entryway, still wearing a frown.

"I found transactions that totaled just over fifty thousand dollars that were processed outside the system—some of them anyway." She leaned her backside against the kitchen counter. "I gave them to Jane."

His jaw dropped as his eyes opened in alarm. "What did you do that for?"

Vanessa caught that look on his face and stormed past him into her office. Maybe she could explain. "I showed it to my boss and explained how Jack had signed the transactions and someone had forged my name on the others. You see, I think he's behind it all. He probably set up Christopher and now he's trying to set me up. You should check into his bank account. I bet you'll find the missing money."

Eric dropped his head and ran his open hand over his face. "I wish you hadn't done that." He walked into the office behind her.

"I know you asked me to back off, but I couldn't. They were about to accuse me of stealing."

"Why won't you listen to me? You're not going to be satisfied until somebody takes a shot at you, are you? I asked you to notify me if you found anything." He didn't give her time to respond to anything as he walked over to her desk and picked up the envelope.

"If you suspect someone at Brightline had something to do with this, why would you take your proof to them and not show it to me first?" He threw the envelope back down with enough force that several other papers flew off the desk.

"But I gave it to Jane. She's cool. She's the only one I trust in that place to help me."

"It doesn't matter. She works for Brightline, doesn't she?"

Vanessa jumped from the couch and went to pick up her papers off the floor. She hadn't seen this side of Eric before. Maybe now he was showing his true colors. "She does, but like I said, Jane's cool."

"How do you know that?"

She threw the papers on her desk and stood facing him with both hands on her hips. "I don't, but she doesn't believe Christopher stole any money, either. Besides, I had to prove the missing money wasn't my fault. I don't want to be thrown in jail for stealing."

Leaning against her desk, Eric folded his arms across his chest. "So that's what this is about? Trying to cover your back. The hell with Christopher. You just want to prove you didn't do anything wrong?"

Her mouth fell open at the same time her hand went up. A reflex caused her to reach out and slap his face. How could he think that? That's not what she meant. The true policeman in him was coming out now.

Eric touched the spot where she'd slapped him. "Guess I hit the nail on the head."

Again, her hand went up, but this time he caught it. He held her wrist tight and brought her hand down.

She wanted to spit fire, she was so mad. As he pulled her hand down, he rose from the desk and moved closer to her. The expression on his face softened. His frown relaxed at the same time his eyelids lowered. He stopped and looked deep into her eyes. She couldn't move. Every time he walked into the room, she found it hard to resist him. No matter how mad she was.

He reached out and pulled her to him until their lips touched. He let go of her wrist and slid his arm around her waist. The seductive touch of his lips made her knees buckle. His other hand moved around her waist, pulling her even closer, until she felt her leg between his. He parted her lips with his tongue and let out a soft moan.

She didn't resist him for one minute. Before she knew it, her hands were moving up his back, caressing his shoulder blades. He kissed her with a hunger she hadn't experienced in a long time. The space between them grew warm. Heat radiated from him, turning her temperature up more than a few notches.

Something vibrated against Vanessa's stomach. She jumped back. Eric's pager went off.

He slowly loosened his grip and let out a heavy sigh.

"Damn." He cursed as he pulled back from her and rested his forehead against hers.

She leaned against him as they regained control of their breathing. Seconds later, the pager went off again. She wanted to grab it and throw it out the window.

Eric planted a soft kiss on her forehead and leaned back against the desk again. He pulled his pager from his belt clip and read the message. "Can I use your phone?"

"Sure, it's there, behind the desk." She pointed to the corner of her desk. "Or there's another one in the kitchen if you need privacy."

"This will be fine." He walked over and picked up the phone. "It's my partner."

Vanessa went into the bathroom to give him some privacy. She closed the door and leaned against it, taking a deep breath. What in the hell was she doing kissing that man? He was a policeman for Christ's sake. She walked over to the mirror and ran her hands through her hair. "Pull yourself together, girl," she chastised herself.

"The guys check out, Sean Gardner, and Jack White. Both have solid alibis."

"Damn, that's what I was afraid of." Eric looked over his shoulder to make sure Vanessa wasn't within earshot.

"You want me to run down the rest of the people in this folder?"

"Yeah, do that."

"Where you at, man?"

Eric didn't want to tell him he was at Vanessa's house. He didn't want to hear how he was getting too close to the case again. "I'm at a friend's. Look, I've got more interviews to follow up on tomorrow. Page me if you get anything good."

"Sure, man. Take it easy, and don't do anything I wouldn't do." Harper chuckled.

"Got no idea what you're talking about, man. Like I said, I'm at a friend's." He hung up and picked up the envelope again.

Whatever Vanessa gave to her boss may have been just the information he needed to prove company embezzlement. All he had to do was get a copy from her. But first, he had to convince her to stop snooping around before she got hurt. Before he had to kill somebody for hurting her.

She walked back into the office and he set down the envelope. The look in her eyes as she crossed the room set his soul on fire. He wanted her in the worst way. And from the intensity of that kiss, he knew she felt the same.

"Eric, I'm sorry I didn't talk with you first. I panicked, and my first reaction was to try and clear my name. You can't blame me for that."

"No, and all will be forgiven if you give me a copy of what you gave her."

She walked close to him, but not close enough. He wanted her between his legs again. Standing close enough so she could feel how much he wanted her. He ran an open hand across his face again, and let out an exasperated sigh. What was happening between them? What was he doing?

"This is gonna sound stupid, but I was in such a hurry, I forgot to make a copy." She smiled with raised brows.

He raised his hand to scold her, but changed his mind. Instead, he put two fingers to each temple and took a deep breath. He decided to change the subject before he lost his cool.

"Forget that. Do you know who Christopher was meeting Friday night?"

"No, how would I know?"

"After he left the club, I believe he got in the car with

somebody and drove off. I don't know what happened after that."

"How do you know he left with anyone?"

"I found somebody who saw him get into an old green car around ten-thirty and drive off. Looks like they brought him back—"

"What kind of old green car?" she asked, paralyzed with fear.

Eric caught the frightened look in her eyes. "An Oldsmobile. Why?"

"I saw an old green Oldsmobile parked across the street one day when I came home. I saw the same car in the parking deck at work."

"Got any idea whose car it is?"

"I think it's Jack's, but I'm not sure."

Eric shook his head. Jack had just been cleared of all wrongdoing, as far as he was concerned. "Are you sure it's Jack's car?"

"No, but this guy told me it might be his."

"Who was that?" Eric reached into his jacket pocket and pulled out a small pad.

"James. He works in accounting. He saw me looking in the car and asked if it was mine. I told him no, then he said he thought it was Jack's."

"What were you doing looking into the car?" This woman must have a death wish, he thought.

"I was trying to tell if it was the same car parked across the street from me or not."

"And you had to look inside for that?"

"No, I suppose not, but—"

"But you couldn't resist." He finished for her. "Do me a favor."

She crossed her arms and leaned on the desk standing next to him, but not close enough for him to pull her in to him. "I'll try."

He gave her a blazing stare. "The next time you see

something that you just have to check out, or you just have to show someone, call me. I've got a feeling this is about to get ugly. If whatever's going on at Brightline was big enough to cost Christopher his life, what makes you think they won't stop anybody else who gets in their way?"

She looked down at the floor like a scolded child. "I was just trying to help."

He reached out and touched her arm. "I know you were and I appreciate that. But it's not safe for you to help any longer. I've got a few days to get something that allows me to keep the case open."

She started to speak, but he stopped her.

"And you will let the police handle everything from here, right?"

She stared down at the envelope on her desk.

He touched her chin with his index finger and slowly brought her face up to meet his. "Right?"

She shook her head.

"Man, I've never met anyone in my life as stubborn as you."

"I'm not stubborn about everything."

He detected a slight seductive pout to her lips. They were poised and waiting for him to possess them. And he wasn't foolish enough to miss this signal. He stood, and closed the distance to possess them. "Thank God, you aren't."

He mentally shut out the angel on his shoulder warning him about getting involved, and kissed her with a hunger that had lain dormant within him for months. A warm serene feeling flowed over his body. A familiar feeling, yet he couldn't put a name to it.

The piercing ring of her phone interrupted them this time. She pulled away first, diverting her eyes from him. He caught her by the arms and turned her back toward him.

"Don't answer it," he pleaded. He wanted to touch, taste, and feel her a little while longer.

The phone rang again.

He reached out and caressed the side of her face, hoping to regain her attention. Needing her back in the depths of his arms.

It rang yet again.

She swayed from side to side before pulling completely from his grip. "I have to." Stepping behind her desk, she reached over and grabbed the phone.

Eric leaned against her desk looking down at himself. Why was he torturing himself this way? He had to get out of there.

"Betty, Betty, stop crying. Honey, I can't understand you." She pulled her chair up and sat on the edge of the seat. "Don't worry, Harold will be back. He's probably just going through something."

Hearing the frantic tone of her voice, Eric turned around. What had happened? Who was Betty?

Vanessa put her hand over the receiver. "It's my sister."

He nodded. "I'm just going to let myself out then."

She stood, holding the phone against her chest. "I'm sorry, Eric. My sister's husband walked out on her and she—"

He held up his hand. "You don't have to explain. I understand. I'll call you tomorrow. Come lock the door."

She followed him to the back door with the phone to her ear. When he turned around to say good night, she reached out and kissed him on the mouth. A brief, yet electrifying kiss.

He walked to his car, tasting her on his lips and knowing now what that warm feeling had been. He was falling in love with Vanessa Benton.

* * *

The next morning Eric walked into Brightline without an appointment, hoping to meet with Vanessa's boss. He needed to see what Vanessa had given her.

Nikki, the secretary, stopped talking at the sight of Eric walking toward her. "Uh-huh, girl, I have to go. I'll call you back later."

"Hello . . . Nikki, is it?"

"Yes. Mr. Steel isn't available right now."

"That's okay, because I'm not here to see him."

"I hope you aren't here to see me?" She pointed to herself.

He chuckled. "No; how about Jane Portman?"

"Oh. She's out today."

"Traveling on business?"

"No, just out. She must be sick or something."

"Can I ask for a favor?"

Nikki sat back and crossed her arms. "Do I have a choice?"

He leaned over, placing both hands on her desk. "Sure you do. But I can't see why you wouldn't want to help me."

"What ya need?"

He reached into his jacket pocket and pulled out a business card. "Give me a call when she comes in, or if she calls in. I need to see her. It's pretty important."

She took the card. "I already have one of these."

"Since you have two, I can be assured that you'll use one this time."

She narrowed her eyes at him, then smiled as Mitch walked up behind him. "I'll do whatever I can to assist."

Eric noticed her slide the card off her desk and into the top drawer. He straightened and turned around.

"Detective Daniels, to what do we owe the pleasure?"

Mitch Waiters—Eric knew who he was. First-level manager, and a man with very little clout. His background was being checked as they spoke. Eric reached out and took the hand extended to him. “I stopped by to see Ms. Portman, but it looks like she’s out today.”

“Yeah, I heard she had to go visit a sick relative out of town.”

Eric glanced over at Nikki, who had turned back to her computer and started typing.

“Any idea when she’ll be returning?”

Mitch shrugged. “From what I hear, it might be days, or weeks—who knows?” He walked up to Nikki’s desk and set down the folder he was holding. “But I’m sure that Nikki here will let you know the minute she returns.”

Nikki gave Eric a spastic smile, then turned back to her computer.

He thanked them and left. Before he reached the car he called Harper on his cell phone and asked what he’d found out on Mitch Waiters.

Eighteen

Friday morning, Vanessa hoped Jane would be back. She could hardly wait to find out what Jane had done about the paperwork she'd given her. Hopefully, an investigation was being launched to find out who forged her name on the documents, and they would have their thief. Which would also clear Christopher's name.

Whether it worked or not, she'd told herself she'd let Eric handle everything from now on. He hadn't given up on trying to find the killer. He was also changing her opinion of policemen, or rather, detectives.

"I guess our meeting this morning is off, huh?" Brenda asked.

"What meeting?" Vanessa asked absently as she kept working.

"It's Friday morning—our weekly staff meeting. Did you forget?"

She looked at her watch. "Oh, yeah. Let's go."

"Jane's not here. I guess it's postponed," Brenda pointed out.

"She's not? She wasn't here yesterday, either. I hope she's okay."

"So do I. I hear she's visiting a sick relative."

"Man, I hate that. I really need to talk to her. How do you know that's where she's at?"

"Nikki told me. Looks like everybody's been looking for her. Even your detective friend."

Vanessa stood. "When was he here?"

"Yesterday. He came by to see Jane. He didn't tell you?"

"Why would he? We don't talk every night or anything. He's the detective on Christopher's case, *that's all,*" she emphasized.

Brenda smiled at her. "I hear you, girl. You don't have to convince me."

Brenda had never seen them together. What was she talking about? Vanessa was sure she hadn't talked about Eric *that* much. She looked up and saw Mitch Waiters walking toward her. *What now?* she thought.

"Vanessa, can I speak to you a moment please?"

"Yes, sir." She stood and shrugged at Brenda once he turned his back. What could he possibly want with her? Mitch was Jane's peer, and rarely visited their floor. She knew this had to be big, or he would have had Nikki call her. He had such a serious look on his face, she hoped it wasn't bad news. Instead of him heading for the elevator, he turned and headed for Jane's office. Maybe she's back and they want to go over the paperwork I gave Jane, she thought. Yes, that had to be it.

Vince Steel, Jane's boss, was seated behind her desk. Seated across the room was a woman whose name she didn't know, but whom Vanessa recognized from human resources. Mitch walked over to stand by the window. Jane wasn't there. Vince motioned for Vanessa to sit down.

"Have a seat."

She sat down with a sinking feeling in the pit of her stomach.

Mitch leaned against the wall with his arms crossed, like he was standing guard. The woman from HR had a piece of paper in her hand, and a stone face.

"Several weeks ago, we did an audit of all the transactions within Jane's group. As you know, money was missing."

All she could do was shake her head as he looked her dead in the eye. *Here it comes.*

"During a recent internal audit we've discovered not only was money missing from your partner's transactions, but from yours as well. There is another seventy-thousand missing now. Unless that money shows up within the next few days, we'll have to take legal action. Take a few minutes, and get whatever you need to out of your desk." He averted his eyes and looked down as if he were reading.

Vanessa's eyes bucked. She couldn't believe her ears.

"Mitch here will escort you out of the building."

"Wait a minute. Am I being fired?" She looked from Vince to Mitch, then to the woman from HR. Not one would look her in the eye.

"I like you, Vanessa, and I'd like to give you a chance to make things right. We have reason to believe—"

"I don't care what you believe. I didn't steal any money. I gave Jane an envelope the other day with proof that we were being set up. Did she show it to you?" She moved to the edge of her seat, staring Vince down.

"Jane is going to be out for a while, and no, she didn't share any information with me before she left. Do you still have that information?"

Damn. "No, I didn't keep a copy."

"That's too bad."

Her mind was racing a mile a minute. They were going to charge her with theft. She'd probably end up in jail, or dead like Christopher. "I have a diskette at my desk. It contains some of the proof I need. Let me get it and show it to you." She stood.

"Mitch, would you help Ms. Benton back to her desk. I'd like to see that diskette. When you return, I also have some papers for you to sign."

She stormed out of the office with Mitch in tow. She wasn't signing anything; they could forget that.

Because Mitch was as tall as her, he walked in step next to her. "You know, if you helped your partner, we'll find out."

"If you mean Christopher, he didn't do anything. I don't know what you're talking about." She never stopped to look up at him. She kept walking.

"If you're so sure of that, why did he kill himself after he was accused?"

She turned the corner and hurried down the aisle to her desk. "How do you know he killed himself?"

He chuckled. "Come on. He was found dead with the gun in his hand."

She gave him an evil look over her shoulder.

He held his hands up in his defense. "I'm not saying that's funny or anything. It was tragic, I agree. I can't understand why you people won't believe it was suicide. The man got caught stealing a lot of money."

Vanessa tried to shake him off and grab the diskette. She pulled open the middle drawer of her desk where she'd thrown the diskette and sifted through it.

Mitch stood a few feet behind her with his arms crossed, humming.

"I know it's here somewhere. Wait a minute." She closed that drawer and tried the top drawer to her left. She took everything out of the drawer in search of the diskette. Her heart started beating wildly. It was gone.

"It's not here. Somebody stole the diskette." She looked up, but Brenda wasn't at her desk. Then she looked back at Mitch.

"I guess we'd better take a walk back down the hall."

"Damn." She threw papers back in the drawer. She marched back down the hall to Jane's office. Time was up. They'd successfully managed to set her up. What was next?

When she walked into the office, Vince and the woman from HR were standing in front of Jane's desk looking over a piece of paper. Vince turned to her as she walked in. He looked up at Mitch, who shook his head.

"Someone stole the diskette from my desk. But if you can get in touch with Jane, I'm sure she can show you the proof I gave her."

"I'm sorry, but as of today you're suspended." He handed Vanessa a piece of paper. "Would you please sign right here?"

"I'm not signing anything because I didn't do anything."

"Ms. Benton, I don't want to do this. That's why we're giving you two weeks to return the money. We realize now that our system is flawed and some changes are in the works. No longer will it be easy for employees to create accounts and embezzle money through them."

"For the last time, I'm being set up."

"Yes, you told us. If you'd just sign this document . . ."

She crossed her arms. "You can speak to my attorney about this. I'm not signing anything, and I do plan to sue."

He set the paper down. "Well, I hate to do this, but, Mitch, will you escort Ms. Benton out of the building?"

Tears welled up in her eyes, but she was determined not one would fall from her face while she stood in that office. Mitch grabbed a box that was standing against the wall, and stood aside as she marched past him. This time he didn't say a word as she went back to her desk and packed up the few belongings she had. She only had a picture of Reggie, and another of herself on the beach in St. Thomas.

As she walked out to the elevator, several people either pointed or waved at her. Brenda stepped off the elevator as the doors opened for Vanessa and Mitch to step on.

"What's going on?" Brenda asked, looking from Vanessa to Mitch.

"They fired me."

Brenda's mouth fell open as she gawked in disbelief at Vanessa. "You have got to be kidding."

Holding up the box in her hand, Vanessa smiled. "Not hardly. Call me later."

Mitch held the elevator door open and the bell began to ring. Vanessa strolled into the elevator.

"Vanessa, I'm so sorry. What's happening to this place? This is ridiculous," Brenda hollered as the door closed.

Vanessa spent the weekend at her sister's house. Each morning they slept in, both unmotivated to get up and do much. Each morning Betty fixed Reggie a bowl of cereal and went back to bed.

After two days of moping around the house, not combing her hair or bathing, Vanessa decided that was enough. Monday morning she got up and fixed a large breakfast for everyone.

Betty walked into the kitchen in her robe with a bonnet on her hair. "What are you doing?"

"I'm fixing breakfast. Go back and get dressed."

"Why?"

Vanessa put the skillet down and pointed the spatula at her sister. "Because we need to get out of this funk we're in. I'm making omelets for everyone. Get dressed and bring my nephew back with you."

A few minutes later, they were all seated at the kitchen table. Vanessa had opened the blinds to finally let a little sunlight in.

"Do you have to do that?" Betty asked, shielding her eyes with her hand.

"Yes. Come on, it's not the end of the world. So what?

You lost your husband, and I lost my job. We'll get through this like we get through everything else."

"Mama, is Daddy lost?" Reggie asked as he played with his omelet.

"No, baby, he's gone to visit a sick friend for a while." She reached over and patted him on the head.

Vanessa shook her head. "Betty, we need to talk."

"I don't want to talk." She dropped her head and looked down at her plate.

Reggie played airplane with his fork instead of eating his omelet. "Honey, are you finished?" Vanessa asked.

He nodded, already halfway out of the seat.

"Okay, go watch your cartoons." She reached over and helped him out of his seat. Before he ran off, she grabbed his arm. "Come here and give Auntie a kiss first."

He squeezed her neck just like she'd shown him, then ran off.

Vanessa sat there staring across the table at her sister. The sister who once had it all. Many days she'd secretively wanted to trade places with Betty. She wanted a husband and a child who'd give her unconditional love.

She couldn't believe that her sister was going to let this be the end of her marriage. Harold had called twice since Vanessa had been there, but Betty wouldn't talk to him. She cried every night about her life being over, but Vanessa knew it wasn't.

"So, what you gonna do?" Vanessa asked, finishing off her breakfast.

"I don't know." Betty let out a long, loud sigh. "I guess I'll have to get a job."

"That's not what I mean and you know it. Are you just going to give up? Or do you want your husband back?"

"Vanessa, I don't know. I don't like what he did to me. I don't like the way he made me feel. Look at me."

She looked up from her plate and pulled back the hair that fell in no particular order around her face.

"All I see are bags under your eyes—nothing that a good night's sleep won't get rid of. Betty, you're a strong woman."

"No, I'm not. I don't know what to do about anything. Harold made all the decisions around here. All I had to do was keep the house clean and figure out what to cook every night."

"Don't forget about Reggie. You raised him. And that takes a strong woman in itself. He's a handful."

That brought a smile to Betty's face. "He's my little pride and joy."

"I know. Girl, you don't give yourself credit for half the things you do around here. If you wanted to, you could survive without Harold."

Betty laughed again. "Hell, I might have to."

"I doubt that. Really, I think you two are just going through a phase. That man adores you. And I know you love him. You two just need to sit down and talk without screaming at each other. You need to listen to him."

That got her attention. "I do listen to him."

Vanessa crossed her arms as if shielding herself. "Betty, sometimes you have a tendency to not let people speak their mind. You're too busy telling them what you want them to do. I know you did me like that for years. And I see you doing it to Harold at times."

"I don't tell him what to do," she declared with her hands on her hips.

"I'm not saying you do. Just maybe you didn't listen to him when he was trying to tell you something."

Betty got up and threw the rest of her omelet in the trash. "No, that little twit got a hold of him. That's what it is."

"Well, are you going to let her steal your husband? Or are you going to fight for him?"

Betty turned and leaned against the sink, looking at Vanessa, her head tilted.

"You can't let someone else determine your destiny." Vanessa got up and walked over to Betty. "This is your life, and you only travel through it one time, that we're aware of anyway. So go for what you want." She grabbed her sister by the shoulders and shook her softly. "Come on, snap out of it. Pull yourself together, woman. You're supposed to be my role model here." She tried not to laugh as Betty's lifeless body shook about.

"If you don't stop it, I'm going to smack the—"

Vanessa let go and threw her hands up. "Letting go, letting go. No need to get violent."

Betty smoothed her hair back and pushed away from the sink. "You look like you're trying to give me a pep talk. Where have you been for the last two days? Hiding out in my guest room." Vanessa sat back down and Betty walked by her snapping her fingers. "Come on, snap out of it." She mocked her little sister.

"My situation's different," Vanessa protested.

"Sure, it is." Betty strolled out of the kitchen calling Reggie as she left.

Vanessa cleared the table. "Well, at least she heard what I had to say." She loaded the dishwasher, still thinking about what Betty had said. She wasn't hiding. She just needed some rest before they carted her off to jail. There was no way she could fight Brightline. If Eric couldn't prove Christopher's innocence by now, what could he do for her? Any day now, she would lose her job and possibly her freedom. No amount of fighting back could help her. That's probably what Christopher had been doing—trying to fight back. It had gotten him killed.

Reggie ran into the kitchen. "Auntie Vanessa, can I have a Popsicle?"

"You just had breakfast."

"I know." He walked over and held on to her leg, rubbing his face into the fabric of her slacks. "But I want one."

She smirked down at him. In two days he'd managed to eat six Popsicles. But what could they hurt?

"Come on." She had to pry him from her leg to walk over and pull a Popsicle from the freezer. She gave it to him. "Man, you sure can eat for such a little thing."

He took the treat and ripped the paper off.

"Do I get a thank-you?" she asked, stooping down to his level.

He wrapped his arms around her neck and kissed her on the cheek. "I wuv you, Auntie." Then he ran out of the kitchen.

She stood with tears in her eyes. She wuved her nephew, too. He was a perfect child. For a little boy he was very affectionate. He'd grow up to be a perfect gentleman, she was sure. But after the next few days she might never see him again. The thought paralyzed her.

Nineteen

After a night of tossing and turning, Vanessa woke early and jumped into the shower. This morning she was on a mission. She stood at the sink drinking a cup of hazelnut creamer with a little coffee added, when Betty shuffled in, still in her robe.

"Where you going so early?"

"I've got a little business to take care of. I'm no quitter, and neither are you. So get dressed and handle your business."

Betty picked a mug off the mug tree and poured herself a cup of coffee. "I don't have any business."

"Wake up, honey. Your husband left you. You might be down, but you're not out. Don't let him get you down like that. Take care of yourself and Reggie. He's your business."

Betty sat at the kitchen table with her cup, holding her forehead in her palm. She sighed. "Yeah, I guess I'd better do something."

"Look, I'll check back with you later. Gotta run."

Vanessa hurried home to change clothes. She still had information on those bogus companies. All she needed to do was find out who their Brightline contact was and maybe she could save herself.

She walked through her house doing everything as fast as she could. She checked the mail, watered the thirsty plant in her kitchen window, then ran upstairs to change. The answering machine was flashing. She checked it before walking into the closet.

The first message was from Eric on Friday afternoon. "Vanessa, when you come in, give me a call." The second message was from Eric. "Vanessa, are you mad at me or something? I know about work. Give me a call."

She peeked out of the closet at the machine. So he knew she was about to go down. If only he'd been able to find out who at Brightline had set Christopher up, everything would be over. He'd tried, she knew. She grabbed a tan pantsuit and a blouse. Standing next to her bed she took off her clothes. The third message was Eric again, this one left on Saturday.

"Vanessa, I'm getting worried. Where are you? You're not answering your cell phone. I know you need to sulk, but if I don't hear from you by Monday morning, I'm sending a car out to find you."

She picked up the phone and left him a voice message so he would know that she was okay. She didn't want to talk to Eric right now. He wouldn't like what she was about to do.

Her heart pounded in her chest as she drove to the Brightline office. In the seat next to her sat a file folder labeled "Research." Today she was determined to find out what she needed to know.

If she played her cards right, she could catch Jack when he went down for his morning coffee. He was part of the eight o'clock club, a group of men who met every morning and went down for coffee together. She always thought that was so stupid, but today she was thankful for the club.

Instead of parking in Brightline's lot, she parked out front in the visitor parking lot. Once inside, she took the elevator down to the first floor. Across from the cafeteria was a small sitting area. Vanessa took a seat and picked up a company newsletter on the table before her. She pretended to read the paper as she looked out for the eight o'clock club. Five minutes later, like clockwork, the elevator doors opened and four men stepped off.

Vanessa held the paper high, not wanting Jack to see her until he couldn't turn away. As they passed her, she dropped the paper and stood.

"Jack," she called as they passed.

He turned around and lost his smile when he saw her. "Vanessa?"

"Yeah. Can I talk to you a minute?"

His buddies all turned and stared at her. She was sure everyone at Brightline knew what she'd been accused of.

"Yeah, sure." He turned back to his buddies. "I'll catch you guys later."

He walked over and took the seat next to Vanessa. "What happened?"

She sat back down and narrowed her eyes at Jack. "I think you know what happened."

He shrugged. "Mr. Steel said that you left the company. Something about missing funds."

"Jack, does ORICA mean anything to you?" She'd ignored his question. She knew Mr. Steel wanted her out anyway.

He looked at her, contemplating as he shook his head. "No. Should it?"

"Yeah, because you signed the authorization for payment."

"I what?" He stopped shaking his head. "That's not one of my accounts. I don't know what you're trying to do, but I didn't authorize anything for that company."

"Are you sure?" She tried to detect if he was lying.

"I'm positive. Where is the company?"

"It's local. Somewhere in the Gwinnett area."

"Well, there you have it. I don't have any local accounts. I promise you I don't know anything about that company."

"Jack, some of the accounts I'm being accused of stealing from have your name on them. If you're not in on it, do you have any idea who might be?"

He jumped up. "Of course not. If you're trying to insinuate something, you can forget it. I'm not in on anything. I do my job and I go home."

"Jack, I'm being set up, and I think you know something. Guess I'll have to talk to the police."

"You go right ahead. I don't have anything to hide."

"We'll see what Jane has to say about that. I gave her some pretty incriminating stuff."

"Jane! Huh—yeah, when and if she returns."

"What do you mean by that?" Now Vanessa stood.

"Nobody's seen her since the middle of last week. Then yesterday, they cleaned out her office, pictures and all. Everything's gone. So I don't think Jane's coming back."

"She can't be gone. She has all my proof." Jane hadn't returned since Vanessa gave her those files. Something wasn't right.

"Jack, do you remember everybody talking about some termination list around the office?" She knew it was more than a termination list, but she didn't know what he knew.

He eyed her skeptically. "Yeah, I remember. Why?"

"Do you know if it exists? I know you know more about that place than you let on, so level with me, please."

He looked up and down the aisle before answering. "Yeah, I heard about it. They say Mr. Eagan keeps the list in his desk drawer."

"Mr. Eagan!"

He nodded his head. "Look, don't say anything, but I'm leaving Brightline next week myself. I already have a new job lined up. Something's going on up there, all right. Be smart, and don't come back."

She apologized to Jack before he ran off to join his friends in the cafeteria.

Vanessa went back to her car, but decided to look for something before leaving. She pulled into the parking deck. Rounding the corner on the first floor, she looked for the old green Oldsmobile, but it wasn't in its usual spot. So if that wasn't Jack's car, whose was it?

With the file folder still in the passenger seat, she picked up her cell phone and dialed the ORICA Services office. If she was lucky, she could reach someone and find out who their Brightline contact was.

She got a recording saying the number was no longer in service. Determined to get to the bottom of at least one account, she took Interstate 85 and headed for Gwinnett County. She took the Jimmy Carter Exit and traveled west until she reached the railroad track. The industrial park was on her right. After turning in, she slowed down and looked for 1603. First of all she didn't see much movement in the area. If the customer's sales office was in this area, they couldn't be getting much business. Most of the lots were fairly empty.

She was getting closer. Stylish red brick buildings faced the street with signs displaying company names. She reached the middle of the 1600 building. There were no addresses above the door, no signs displaying the company names—nothing.

"This has to be it," she said aloud as she pulled up to the front door and parked. She got out of her car and walked up to the door but didn't see anyone. She pressed her face to the glass and shielded her eyes against the sun for a better look. The office was empty. Not one desk or chair inside.

Backing up, she noticed the grassy area around the door was overgrown and several rolled-up papers were at the foot of the door. She picked one up. A menu from a local Chinese restaurant lay on the ground so long, the paper had yellowed.

A young man walked out of the business next door. Vanessa looked up at the company name above the door and noticed the same logo on his shirt.

"Excuse me." She dropped the menu and walked over to him. He stopped and looked at her. "Can you tell me how long this office has been abandoned?"

He chomped on his chewing gum and reached into his pocket for his keys. "I've never seen anybody over there. And I've been working here for a little over a year. Before then, I can't tell you."

A year. "Thank you."

"Sure." He opened his car door and started to get in.

"Excuse me." She walked over to his door. "I'm sorry, but do you know if the mailman ever delivers there?"

He shook his head. "Who to? Whoever owns the place probably has a post office box somewhere. You thinking about buying the place?"

She shook her head. "No, I was looking for ORICA Services. That's supposed to be their office."

He nodded. "Never heard of 'em. Sorry."

"That's okay. Thanks. Didn't mean to hold you up."

"No problem." He got into his car and drove off.

Vanessa got back into her car and, gripping the steering wheel, looked up at the building. This was the only address she'd found for the company. If the checks weren't being mailed here, where were they going?

Eric pulled most of his proof together, and wanted to discuss it with Chief Torello. He needed to check out one more thing. The body had been discovered at six in the morning by Wayne Pinskey. Eric read the interview conducted by his predecessor, but he wanted to conduct his own interview. He found Mr. Pinskey hustling around Zephyrhill, the restaurant he managed.

"But I told them everything I know. I found the guy slumped over the wheel, that's it."

"Yes, sir, I read the statement you gave to the first detective. I'm new to the case so I just wanted to talk to everybody myself. I've only got a few questions for you, if you don't mind."

Wayne gave a passing waiter a few orders, then turned to Eric. "Sure, let's sit over here." He motioned to a small table in the back.

Eric followed him, pulling out his small pad.

"So, what you wanna know?"

"How about starting when you noticed the car?"

"Well, I came in early cause I had a shipment coming in. I notice this car sitting out front when I first came in, but I didn't notice anybody inside. Then when I walked back out to meet the truck, I noticed this guy sitting there."

"Was he there the first time?"

"I'm sure he was. I just didn't notice. Then I see this guy's leaning forward." He leaned forward, placing his forearms on the table.

"I tell my truck driver to hold on while I go over and check it out. I thought maybe the dude was sick or something. When I got next to the car I saw the blood all over the place. That's when I ran back in here and called the police."

"Did you see anybody around, walking or anything?"

He shook his head. "Na."

Another damned dead end.

"I guess that guy pulled up sometime that morning to kill himself, huh?"

"No, he was at the sports bar down the street the night before."

"Then he must have come back."

"What are you talking about?"

"When I closed up the night before, that car wasn't parked out there."

"Are you sure?"

"Yeah, now that I think of it, I stood outside talking to my manager for about fifteen minutes. If that car had been there, we would have noticed it."

Eric shook his head absently. How long had it been sitting there before it was discovered? And when the kid at the Waffle House saw Christopher leave, did he come back to get his car, then return hours later and kill himself? None of it made sense.

A loud banging noise came from the kitchen, followed by streams of profanities.

"If you're finished with me . . ." Wayne pointed to the kitchen door.

"Sure, go ahead. And thanks." Eric got up and walked out. He stood outside looking at the spot Christopher's car had been parked in. He had to have moved his car, then returned, but why?

Back in his office, Eric picked up Vanessa's message that she was all right. He'd known all along she was at her sister's house. Which was fine with him. She'd been out of the way for a few days. Just enough time for him to get what he needed from Brightline, without her knowing.

He picked up the phone to call her house. According to one of his black-and-whites, she left her sister's early that morning.

"Hello."

"Where you been?" he asked abruptly.

"And hello to you, too."

"I'm sorry. How you doing?"

"As well as can be expected. I'm sure you already know what happened."

"Yeah, I heard. I talked to Mr. Steel the day you left."

"So when are the cops coming to pick me up?"

"He hasn't reported it yet."

"Why not?"

"He claims he's giving you time to turn in the money."

"But I don't have the damned money. You know that. I gave Jane proof that it's a setup, and now she's gone. I've tried to duplicate it, but—"

"What do you mean she's gone?"

"They said she went to visit a sick relative, but when I saw Jack today, he said they cleaned out her office yesterday."

"Where did you see Jack?"

She didn't say anything. *Damn, this woman is going to be the death of me.* He wanted to be upset with her, but he understood the position she was in. If he was close to going to jail, he'd do everything he could to help himself. Still, he wished she realized the seriousness of this case. Even moreso now that he had more evidence.

"Did you go down there today? No, don't tell me. I don't think I want to know the answer to that. Look, I need to ask you a few questions. Will you be home tonight?"

"Yeah."

"I'll come by as soon as I get off, if it's okay."

"Sure, I'll be waiting."

And she couldn't wait. Vanessa hung up, changed clothes and started cleaning the house. If Eric knew about her job, he didn't sound concerned. Then maybe she wasn't about to be carted off to jail after all.

Eric grabbed his folder on the Harris case and prayed he had enough evidence for his boss to keep the case open. He stood, and as he turned around, Harper called out, "Catch," before tossing a package at his stomach.

"Wow, what's this?" Eric asked as he squeezed his stomach muscles and grabbed the package.

"Don't know. It just came for you."

He put the folder down and examined the FedEx package. It had been addressed to him, with no return address. Just like the one Vanessa had received. He flipped it over again. How could it have been sent with no return address?

"Harper, where did you get this?"

"Front desk. When I walked by, they asked me to bring it up to you. I don't know when it came in. Why, what's up?"

"No return address." Eric eyed his partner as he sat back down and ripped it open.

"So no way to track it," Harper commented.

"FedEx didn't deliver it. Somebody else brought this in." Eric pulled out a stack of papers with a big rubber band tied around them. Attached to the papers was a page from a calendar. He pulled it from the rubber band. Then a small cassette tape tumbled from the bag and onto his desk. Eric looked over at his partner, who arched a brow at him.

The calendar page was from April 24th, the day Christopher Harris died. At the bottom of the page, circled, was the name Ronnie. Under it, Dugan's 10:00 P.M. was circled.

"Everything okay?" his partner asked.

Eric shook his head and smiled. "Everything's copacetic." He picked up the tape and pitched it to Harper. "A little present. Let's find a tape recorder."

Twenty

"That's him."

"Who?" Harper asked.

Eric stood and threw his pencil back down on the table. "Ronald Walsh. He works in accounting at Brightline. Now that surprises the hell out of me."

"You sure that's him?"

Eric shook his head, smiling. "I recognize the lisp. That's him, all right."

"Want me to pick him up?"

"You bet." Eric leaned back in his seat. "He processed the checks for those bogus accounts of Christopher's and Vanessa's. I've got a lot of questions for Mr. Walsh. Like, did Christopher leave with him, or come back with him?"

"I'll grab a black-and-white and pick him up now."

"Great. Don't mention the tape. Just bring him in for questioning."

"Detective Daniels, here's those reports you asked for. One on Brightline, and another on Sean Gardner." A first-year detective handed Eric his report.

"That was fast. Thanks, Tucker."

Eric opened the file on Sean first. He looked for something to tell why he hadn't sat down and talked to the police after his lover died. Financially, he was set. He owned a condo in Atlanta, the house in Alabama, and rental property in Miami's South Beach area. Not to mention the numerous investments.

But something else interested Eric more than his financials. Sean had been arrested in Chicago three years ago, for soliciting a police officer. A male police officer.

"Man, oh, man" was all Eric could say. He shook his head and kept reading. Back in 1990, Sean was brought in for questioning when a local Chicago teen was murdered. The young man had been turning tricks, and Sean was listed as a possible john and suspect. After extensive questioning, he was dropped from the list of suspects. The case was still open.

Eric found a little bit of everything but the pesky parking tickets Sean told him about. He also found what he was looking for. Sean may have been afraid to speak to the police.

Now he opened the folder on Brightline. Before he could finish skimming the first page, his phone rang.

"Detective Daniels," He hoped it was his anonymous caller again. He could use more information.

"Daniels, this is Officer Ryan from the state police office. I'm afraid I've got some disturbing news for you."

Disturbing news—Eric didn't like those two words. And what did the state police want with him? "Officer Ryan, what could I be working on that you guys would be interested in?"

"It's actually the other way around. We've found something that might have something to do with a case you're working on. Do you know a Jane Portman?"

"Yes, I do." He didn't want to share his information with the state police.

"This morning, some freeway workers found her car off the side of the road in Jasper, Tennessee. Looks like she might have fallen asleep at the wheel, or been forced off the road. We're not sure yet, but she's dead."

Eric dropped his head. “Damn. Look, can you page me as soon as you have more information?”

“Sure. I’ll get back to you in a little while.”

Eric hung up and closed the folder in front of him. Now he had to check on Vanessa and let her know what happened before she heard it from somewhere else and freaked out.

He checked in with Harper on his way to Vanessa’s.

“How’s it going with Walsh?”

“So far, no luck. He wasn’t at home, at work, or at the gym that I’ve been told he goes to every evening. We’ll keep looking, and I’ll page you as soon as I get him.”

“We’ve got a new development, so I’m gonna run by Vanessa’s. . . .”

“Any excuse will do,” Harper teased.

“I’m going to deliver bad news. Her boss was found dead this morning.”

“Wow! Sorry, dude. Need me to follow up on any details?”

“Yeah, check everything out for me.” Eric gave Harper the state trooper’s name so he could see if the death had anything to do with the case. Then he continued to Vanessa’s house.

Vanessa opened the front door. “Mad at me?” she asked.

“No.” Eric walked past her with his shoulders slumped.

She detected something wasn’t right. “What is it?”

“Come on and sit down.”

She closed the front door and followed him into the living-room. He sat on the couch. She tucked one foot underneath her, and sat next to him.

"I'm sorry, but Jane Portman's body was found this morning in Jasper, Tennessee."

Vanessa shot straight up in her seat. "Oh my God! You're kidding."

Eric shook his head. "I don't know exactly what happened yet, but she may have fallen asleep at the wheel."

"Are you sure? I just can't believe it."

"I'm waiting on more information. I'm afraid it's true."

A large knot grew in her throat. She tried to swallow and almost threw up. "You don't think it was the same thing that happened to Christopher, do you?"

They looked at each other. Vanessa could see in Eric's eyes he thought the same thing. "Who is doing this?" she screamed.

He turned in his seat and grasped her hand. "Vanessa, tell me what happened at Brightline today."

She wiped at the tears slowly falling from her eyes. "I talked to Jack, but I don't think he's involved, after all."

"Vanessa, I've got something to say, and I want you to listen to me this time."

"I'm listening."

"No, Vanessa." He took her chin in his head and forced her to look up into his eyes. "I mean *really* listen."

He'd never looked so serious before. She shook her head. "I'm listening," she said, softer this time.

"Ronnie met Christopher that Friday night at Dugan's. We sent a car out to pick him up, but he's gone."

"Are you trying to tell me Ronnie killed Christopher?" Her eyes widened in alarm. There had to be a mistake. Ronnie wouldn't hurt a flea.

"I won't know until I talk with him, but he's looking like our man. That's why I needed to talk with you. How close was he to Christopher?"

She shrugged. "They went to lunch together every now and then. From time to time Ronnie would have a problem with an address, and get Christopher's help, but nothing else that I know of." She wiped at the tears still trailing down her cheek. "However, he did tell me the other day he could help me with Christopher's work. I wondered myself how close they were. But I don't think he could kill him."

"Are you sure? Think hard. He met with Christopher the night he died, but didn't mention it when he was interviewed."

"How do you know they met?"

Eric sat back. "Somebody sent me the tape from Christopher's answering machine this morning. I'm going to assume it was Sean. I tried to reach him, but he's out of town and I couldn't get the number."

Vanessa got up and paced around the room with her arms crossed. "I just can't believe this. Not Ronnie. Not Jane! What's going on at that place?" She began crying again.

Eric got up and stopped her in front of him. He ran his hands up her arms and slid them around her back. "Hey, don't cry."

"I wasn't scared before, but I'm scared now. Will I be next?" She sniffled as he held her against his chest.

"Don't talk like that. I won't let anything happen to you."

She pulled back from him and looked up into his eyes. Right now, she was doing something she never thought she'd do again. Trusting a cop.

"You promise?"

"I promise," he said barely above a whisper.

The smoldering look in Eric's eyes came closer as he gently kissed her forehead. She closed her eyes and felt the soft kisses trailing down her face to her neck.

"I love your neck," he softly whispered in her ear.

A soft moan escaped her lips. Her skin tingled from his touch. His warm breath against her neck at first caused all her senses to stand at attention, then it tickled. She couldn't help but giggle. "Stop, I'm ticklish."

"Does this tickle?" he asked before placing his lips over hers. He took a step forward, engulfing her into the folds of him.

She slowly brought her arms up his back, pressing her body against his. He was a few inches taller than her, which equaled a perfect fit. His hungry mouth brought to the surface desires she thought were long buried. Her body responded to him like a hungry baby waiting to be fed. Her nipples hardened as her chest rubbed against his. The hunger between her legs screamed to be fed.

His kisses moved from her face to her neck and back to her face. Ever so slowly, he savored each kiss as if it would be his last. The seductive kisses were driving her over the edge. Her body was one big fireball. She closed her eyes and thought about all the times at night alone in her bedroom when she dreamed about him.

His kisses subsided and he took a slow step back, looking down into her eyes. "What am I doing?" he asked with his arms still around her.

"It's called kissing," she said humorously, trying to catch her breath.

He chuckled and pulled her back into his arms. "Can you feel that?"

Was she dreaming, or did he ask her if she noticed his erection? "Feel what?"

"My heartbeat."

She let out a soft sigh. "I thought that was *my* heart beating so hard and fast."

He leaned back and took her face in his hands. With his thumbs, he slowly wiped under her eyes where tears lay moments ago.

"Eric, I really am scared."

"Don't worry. Nothing's going to happen to you. As soon as we find Ronald Walsh, we'll have some answers. Besides, I wouldn't let anybody hurt you. I've had a car on you ever since someone broke in here."

She blinked. "You've had me followed?"

"Only to make sure nobody tried to hurt you."

"Why didn't you tell me?"

"For what? So you could tell me not to? In case you don't realize it, you're a little stubborn." He kissed the tip of her nose.

"I don't know if I like that or not."

"Vanessa, I asked you to leave the detective work to me. You didn't, so I had to make sure you didn't get hurt in the process."

"Then I guess I should thank you."

"You really want to thank me?"

Before she could respond, he captured her mouth again, this time kissing her with more passion and hunger than before. Now he was the baby begging to be fed.

Vanessa didn't want to protest or come to her senses. She wanted to go with the moment, to act on the lust and want she felt for this man.

His beard was so close-shaven, it wasn't much more than a shadow. But she liked it. She liked the way he was so smooth. When he walked across the room, he looked so smooth. The way he'd grabbed her to kiss her, and how he held on to her was so smooth. His hands caressed her back, gently massaging her into a relaxed sensual state.

He adjusted his head to the right and kept ravishing her mouth. He tasted like peppermint. Suddenly, she loved the taste of peppermint. She couldn't get enough of it.

Together they moved from a standing position to sitting on the couch. Still embraced, her arms traveled up and around his neck. She caressed the back of his neck with her fingertips.

Eric trailed down the side of her neck planting small kisses along the way. She bit her bottom lip as his hand caressed her breast. He touched her, but she wanted to feel his hand against her bare skin.

Her body was on fire. Eric stopped kissing her long enough to unbutton her blouse, and slowly slid it off her shoulders. He kissed her bare shoulders as the blouse fell away. She leaned back on the couch, still caressing the back of his neck as his lips brushed down her shoulder to her breast.

As he kissed along her cleavage, Vanessa lowered herself even more until she was stretched out on the couch. Eric followed as if he were unable to let go. Their feet hung off the edge of the couch, and she kicked off her shoes.

Vanessa came to her senses when he unsnapped the front of her bra. His hot breath against her breast caused her eyes to shoot wide open. Then the cool sensation as his tongue glided over her nipple caused them to flutter closed again.

"Eric, what are we doing?" she asked between ragged breaths.

He rose, looking down at her breast. Then he looked into her eyes as he brought his breathing back to normal. "Something I've wanted to do since you walked into that interview room." He pulled her up into a sitting position, then all the way up on her feet.

Vanessa stood there with her bra open, catching a draft and feeling like a horny teenager. Her blouse dropped to the couch as she stood.

"Come on." Eric took her hand and led her to the foot of the stairs. He stopped and looked back at her.

Vanessa walked past him, kissing him on the way. She took his hand and led him up the steps to her bedroom.

As soon as she stepped through the door he grabbed her, slid his arm around her waist, and turned her to face him. He pushed her bra back until it fell off her shoulders and hit the floor.

Hot and too bothered for words, Vanessa helped Eric out of his clothes while he helped her out of hers. Sitting on the edge of the bed he took a deep breath. For a minute, she thought he was about to get dressed and leave.

"This isn't going to be easy, you know?"

"Why? What's wrong?" Did he have some sort of problem that he needed to tell her about?

"My life can be kind of difficult."

"Oh, that's what you mean. I know. I've kind of been there before."

He turned to her and caressed her cheek with the back of his hand. "I don't believe in one-night stands."

She looked up into his eyes. "Neither do I."

Eric jumped up in bed, his senses on alert. He heard something. He wiped his eyes as the room came into focus. The soft yellow walls and curtains on the windows reminded him that he wasn't at home. The covers were pushed to the foot of the bed. He looked from Vanessa's long legs up over the curve of her hips to her beautiful round breast.

No going back now. He couldn't wait until the case was solved to get involved with her. He'd tried; he really had. But something kept bringing them together.

He snapped his head around toward the bedroom door. He heard it again. Reaching for his pants he smelled something. He sniffed the air a few times. Kerosene.

"Vanessa, Vanessa." He shook her, pulling her from a deep sleep. He glanced at her, a quick picture of their earlier lovemaking firm in his mind, before pitching her clothes to her.

"Huh?" She rolled over, moaning.

"Put them on." He grabbed his gun and ran out of the bedroom. She'd be okay until he checked everything out. Standing at the top of the stairs he smelled smoke.

He ran back into the bedroom. Vanessa sat on the side of the bed putting her pants on.

"Come on, baby. We've got to get out of here." He took her hand and pulled her out of the room as she pulled a T-shirt down over her breasts.

"What's going on?" she asked, still trying to wake up.

"Hurry." The stairway looked clear so he ran down the stairs.

"What's that smell?" Vanessa, fully awake now, ran down behind him, beginning to panic.

At the foot of the stairs, they saw the fire spreading across the living room couch, starting up the curtains.

"Do you have a fire extinguisher?"

"Yeah, it's under the sink in the kitchen." She pointed toward the kitchen as Eric opened the front door and tried to push her out.

He ran back into the kitchen, pulled open the cabinet under the sink, but didn't see anything. He turned to run and call Vanessa.

"It's there in the back." She was right behind him.

"What are you doing in here? Get out of the house," he yelled at her as he pulled out the extinguisher. In the living-room, the fire had traveled the length of the couch, completely torched the curtains, and was working its way out of a corner.

Eric pulled the pin on the extinguisher and walked closer to the fire. He emptied the extinguisher, but the fire still burned.

"Here, take this one!" Vanessa called from behind him.

She held out another extinguisher. He quickly took it and doused the fire. Smoke filled the air, choking them. He grabbed her hand as they walked outside, crouching to clear their lungs.

Seconds later, a fire truck pulled up. Eric went back upstairs and grabbed his shirt and badge. Vanessa sat on the front steps with her knees to her chest rocking herself.

"Are you okay?" he asked as the firemen went inside to check everything out.

"Yeah, I'm okay. I guess."

He sat next to her and put his arm around her shoulders. He kissed her on the cheek. "You're a dangerous lady to be around, do you realize that?"

She reached over and punched him playfully in the side. "Don't say that. What happened to the guy you had watching me?"

Eric leaned back against the step and sighed. "I sent him home since I was here."

She looked back at him. "Thank God you were here."

"I told you I'm not going to let anything happen to you."

She took a deep breath and placed her hands over her face and began to cry. Eric placed his hand on her back, caressing her as he let her get it out of her system.

"Don't worry, I'll find out who did this." Her cries became harder and he wrapped his arms around her, pulling her into his chest.

A car came flying down the street and stopped in front of Vanessa's house. The car door opened, and Harper stepped out. He ran up the steps to where Vanessa and Eric were sitting.

"I got here as fast as I could, man. What happened?"

"Somebody threw something flammable through the window. The fire department's checking it out. I'll know what it was in a few minutes."

"Did you see who it was?" he asked Vanessa.

She looked up at him, but Eric answered, "No, she was asleep." He still held Vanessa as her tears subsided.

Harper looked down at Eric's bare feet, then at his watch. "Looks like it just happened. Were you here?"

Eric stared at him, knowing he had to answer, but not sure if he was ready for the lecture. Not now. He partially closed his eyes. "Yeah, I was still here."

Harper snorted. "Huh, guess I should be asking you, did you see anybody?"

"No, I just heard a noise. My guess is it was the window breaking. I was asleep."

"Asleep!" Harper nodded.

Eric wished this night hadn't turned out so disastrous. Vanessa's neighbors were peeking out of their doors and windows.

"Looks like somebody sent you a little Mol cocktail," the fireman said as he stepped out the front door. "Good thing you had those fire extinguishers. They might have saved your life tonight."

She looked up at Eric. "Thank you. I'm alive tonight, all because of you."

Eric looked up at Harper. He stood there with his hands deep into his pockets. "I'll go talk to the firemen." Harper walked past them into the house.

Eric kissed Vanessa on her forehead.

Twenty-one

"There. I'm finished, but it doesn't sound like much." Betty pushed back from the computer, throwing up her arms in frustration.

"Let me see." Vanessa picked up the paper as it came off the printer.

"Who am I fooling? Nobody's going to hire me. I have a marketing degree and not one day's worth of experience. I meant to get a job—I always did—but then Harold came along and he didn't want me to work."

"Well, you have to work now." Vanessa scanned the résumé. "This looks good. What time is your appointment?"

"One o'clock. Wish me luck."

The phone rang as Vanessa handed back Betty's résumé. "Good luck, not that you'll need it. You won't have a problem."

"Let's hope not." Betty reached over and grabbed the phone on the second ring.

"It's for you." She shrugged as she handed Vanessa the phone, indicating she didn't know who it was.

"Vanessa, are you all right?" It was Brenda.

"Brenda? Yeah, I'm fine."

"I heard about the fire last night, so I figured you might be there. Is everything okay?"

Vanessa pointed to the phone and mouthed the word "Brenda," so Betty would know who she was talking to.

"Aside from the fact that my living room was toasted, everything else is okay."

"Girl, I couldn't believe it. Do you have any idea who did it?"

"Not yet. Detective Daniels is looking into it." He heard the crash and had smelled the kerosene before she did. But she wasn't telling Brenda that.

"Well, thank God you're okay."

"Yeah. I'm surprised you heard about it so fast."

"Girl, lately, this place has become a gossip mill. I'm sure your detective friend told you about Jane, didn't he?"

"He did, but, Brenda, I don't believe that accident story for one minute."

"Neither do I. I've been scared to say that to anyone, but it doesn't sound right, does it?"

"No, it doesn't. Especially because it happened right after I gave her the paperwork to prove I'd been set up."

"Do you think she got a chance to show it to anyone?"

"I don't know, but I hope so."

"Well, I just wanted to say I'm sorry to hear about the fire. It was probably some young thugs."

Vanessa doubted that. She walked over and peeked out the window at the unmarked car parked across the street. The police officer inside nodded his head at her.

"Yeah, probably so."

"Now, girl, if you need anything, just give me a call. Your sister lives out in Kennesaw, right?"

"Yeah, Brenda. Thanks a lot, but I gotta run. I'll give you a call in a day or two to let you know if, and when, I'll be back in."

"Hey, you do that. Don't go and disappear on me. We're buddies, remember?"

"Don't worry, I'm not going anywhere." And she meant that.

After hanging up, Vanessa looked at the kitchen clock.

It was eight o'clock in the morning, and she needed to know if she had a job to go to or not. Her time limit to return the money was up, but Mr. Steel hadn't called.

She paced the kitchen, not knowing what to do. Eric had told her to sit tight until he called, but she'd never been able to sit tight a day in her life. She needed to know something.

Reggie was in the den watching television and Betty was in the shower. Vanessa jumped at the opportunity to have some quiet time to make a phone call. The suspense was driving her crazy. Either Brightline was going to charge her or not.

Nikki answered the phone in her usual singsong voice. "Hello, Brightline. How may I help you?"

"Nikki, this is Vanessa. Is Mr. Steel in?"

"Oh, hello, Vanessa. I've been trying to call you all morning. Hold please."

Here we go. This is it. Were they just going to fire her, or have her arrested?

"Vanessa, your call is right on time." A voice deeper than Mr. Steel's came on the line.

"Mitch! Is Mr. Steel not in?" She didn't want to discuss anything with him. He was one man that she'd never really liked. Anything he could lay on his employees, he would. The man had no backbone.

"He's unavailable right now. Are you coming in this morning?"

"I'm afraid not. There was a little accident at my house last night."

"I'm sorry to hear that. I hope no one got hurt?"

"No, luckily everyone is fine."

"That's good." He hesitated a moment before asking, "Do you have something for us?"

"I'd like to speak with Mr. Steel."

"Do you know what the charge is for stealing seventy thousand dollars?"

"I'm telling you, I didn't steal that money."

"You're forcing us to press charges. Mr. Steel is prepared to—"

"Go ahead, press your charges. You'll be talking to my lawyer." She slammed the phone down, then held up her hand, watching it shake. My God, she was going to jail. Fear ripped through her body so fast, she had to sit down. She didn't have a lawyer.

"What's going on?" Betty asked when she walked into the kitchen all made up and dressed in a sundress.

"They're pressing charges."

"You're kidding!"

"I wish." She grabbed the phone again. "I've got to get Eric."

Betty stood by the kitchen sink with her hands over her mouth as, in horror, she watched her little sister. "We've got to get you a good lawyer. I'll make some calls."

"Hello, I need to speak with Detective Daniels."

"I'm sorry, he's unavailable right now. May I take a message, or would you like his voice mail?"

"Voice mail, please." She left a brief, but urgent, message.

"Page him. You've got the number, don't you?" Betty asked.

Vanessa snapped her fingers and pointed at her sister. "Thank you, Betty. I don't know what I'm thinking. Where did I put my purse?" She ran off into the other room, looking for her purse. "Oh, Eric, where are you?"

Eric sat facing Ronnie. The table in the interrogation room moved against the wall. Harper sat on the edge of the table. A huge folder sat next to him. He'd told Ronnie Walsh the folder contained information they had learned on him. Enough to convict, they lied.

"You guys were more than friends, weren't you?" Eric stood and paced behind Ronnie, watching him rub his hands up and down the thigh of his slacks.

"I don't know what you mean. We worked together."

"We know Christopher was gay, Ronnie. You don't have to pretend with us. So he wasn't out of the closet. Maybe you aren't, either."

Ronnie shook his head looking down at the floor. "I don't know what he wath, but I ain't no damn fag."

He shot Eric a nasty look. The same look Eric might have given someone if they had accused him of the same thing. *But then, you never know,* he thought.

"Ronnie, I know you killed him. So make it easy on yourself and tell me what happened."

"Hold on, man. I met Chrithopher to talk about work, that's it. I'm not a murderer. We had to work out a little problem."

"Meaning what?" Eric asked.

Eric and Harper shared a questioning glance. Harper walked over to lean against the door as if he was holding it up.

"A little trouble at work." Ronnie tilted his head to the left and shrugged.

Eric's patience was wearing thin. He walked over and slammed his hand on the desk. "I want to know exactly what your meeting with Christopher Harris was all about. Did you kill him?"

"Hell, no!" Ronnie jumped up from his seat.

Eric placed his hand on Ronnie's shoulder and shoved him back into his seat. "Then you'd better start talking. I've got a dead guy and a taped conversation of your rendezvous." His pager went off. He glanced down to see Vanessa's sister's number. No time to call her right now.

"I told you I met him to talk about work. Thingth hadn't been going good lately."

Eric threw his hands up and walked toward Harper. "I don't have time to play with him. Lock him up."

"What for?" Ronnie asked, leaning so far forward, he almost fell out of his seat.

Harper pulled a pair of cuffs out of his pocket. "Okay, I'll take care of him."

Eric opened the door to leave.

"Okay, okay. It wath about the money. The mithing money from Brightline."

Holding the door open, Eric stopped and looked back over his shoulder at Ronnie.

Ronnie looked up at Harper holding the cuffs in his hand. "I'm not lying, man." He directed his stare back at Eric. "But if I tell you, I'm a dead man."

Eric walked back in and closed the door. He kicked his chair around to a different position and sat back down.

"Start talking." Eric motioned for Harper to back off. He walked back over to the table, putting his cuffs away.

Wiping the perspiration from his forehead, Ronnie slumped down in his seat. "Chrithopher called me about transactions that I procethed. He wanted to know where they'd been mailed." Ronnie looked over to make sure Harper wasn't holding the cuffs out on him any longer.

"Keep talking," Eric said.

Taking a deep breath and sitting upright in his seat, Ronnie laid both forearms across the table and pleaded with Eric. "Detective, you don't underthand. What I'm about to tell you will coth me my life. Can you protect me?" He glanced at Harper again.

"Let me hear what you've got first. You haven't told me a damned thing yet."

"Naw, man, I want witneth protection or something. If I talk, I want to know that the police will protect me. Move me to another thtate."

Eric got up and walked away to keep from laughing.

This guy had watched too much television. He caught Harper's eye and they both chuckled. "Why don't you tell me what you know, and we'll work something out?"

"Like witneth protection?"

Pivoting his head left then right, Eric shrugged. "Something like that, yeah."

Ronnie looked from one detective to the other before giving in. "He found out that the checks were being mailed to another poth office box, and not the addreth posted on the checks."

"What checks?"

"A couple of the s-special handling accounth I mail out." After placing his elbow on the table, Ronnie dropped his forehead into the palm of his hand. "I'm juth doing my job, man."

"I need to know which accounts, and where you mailed them to."

Ronnie threw himself back into the seat and stared up at the ceiling. A look of doom encompassed his face. "W.B., Neetlebutterth, and ORICA." He took a deep breath then exhaled.

Eric had pulled out a pad and tapped his eraser against the pad. "All accounts set up by Brenda Singleton, right?"

Ronnie's head snapped up and he gave Eric an incredulous stare. He slowly nodded his head.

"So are you and Brenda in this together? Is that why you killed Christopher? He found out?"

Ronnie dropped his head.

Unable to reach Eric by phone or pager, Vanessa got dressed and went in search of him. On the way to the police station, she found herself turning off the expressway and heading for Brightline.

She knew her days were numbered, so why not try

the only thing she thought she had left? If she could just show Mr. Steel everything she'd found, maybe he'd think it was enough to suspect someone else. At this point, she didn't know whom to suspect. All along she thought Jack was the thief. But after talking with him, she wasn't sure anymore.

Instead of marching in through the double glass doors, and giving Nikki time to notify Mitch that she was in the building, Vanessa went around to the service entrance. She figured her badge was probably deactivated by now, so she didn't even try it. Right away, she saw two of the cleaning guys from her floor. She'd always been friendly to the maintenance workers of the building. Surely they hadn't heard about what had happened with her.

"Hello, Juan."

Surprised to see her in the area, the young Mexican man gave her a wide-eyed smile. "Vanessa, good morning."

She thought fast, trying to come up with an excuse to have him let her into the building. "Juan, I need a favor."

"Sure. What can I get you?"

"I've got a very important meeting this morning, and I lost my badge."

He glanced down at his badge, then around to see if anyone was watching them. "Why don't you just get a visitor's badge?"

"Juan, if you could let me in, I'd appreciate it. This is the third time I've lost it, and they're going to want to charge me to make another one. I know it's around my house somewhere and I can find it after work. Trust me. I won't tell a soul you helped me."

He backed up toward the door and ran his swipe card through. She thanked him and passed quickly. "Sure thing" was all he said as he closed the door and kept working.

She took the stairs in order to avoid Nikki, but once she reached the eighteenth floor she'd have to worry about getting in again.

As she turned the corner on the fourth floor she heard what sounded like horses charging down the stairs. When she stopped to listen, she realized it was some women who worked with her. Every morning they put on their tennis shoes and took the stairs to the first floor and back up for exercise. She'd found her way in.

After she talked the girls into letting her in, she headed straight for Mr. Steel's office. The door was open and he sat behind the desk looking down at some papers. Vanessa quietly walked in and closed the door behind her.

Vince Steel looked up and took his glasses off once he noticed Vanessa.

Before he could ask her to leave, she hurried to say what she had to. "Mr. Steel, I'm sorry for barging in like this, but I have to talk to you."

"I'm sorry, Ms. Benton, but I have a conference call in just a minute so you'll have to come back. Did Nikki let you in here?"

"No, sir, I came up the stairs. Mr. Steel, I'm not leaving until I show you something." She set her purse down and walked over to lay the manila folder on his desk.

"What's this?"

"Sir, somebody has stolen money from Brightline, but it wasn't me." She unfolded an 11 x 12 spreadsheet. "If you'll look right here, you can see most of the transactions that make up the missing hundred and twenty thousand dollars. The fifty thousand Chris is accused of taking and the seventy thousand I've been accused of taking. Then here"—she pulled out a few more papers and laid them before him—"you can see the accounts were signed off by Jack, not Christopher or myself."

He put his glasses back on and scanned over the spreadsheet before picking up the papers and reading over them.

"I can't tell you who did the initial setup on the accounts, or where the money went, but I know it wasn't mailed to these companies."

He looked from the paper to her, nodding his head. "How do you know that?"

"The companies don't exist. None of them do."

"What would you say if I told you I already know that much? My question to you is, where is the money?"

"Sir, if you find out who sent out those checks, you've got your man, or woman. They probably mailed them to a post office box somewhere to pick them up later."

"Hmm," He appeared to be thinking as he walked from behind his desk to the door. He opened the door and peeked out.

"This is what I tried to show you before."

"Is this the evidence you showed Jane?" He closed the door and returned to his desk.

"I showed her much more than this. I had exact amounts, dates, and everything. My signature was forged on the paperwork. Christopher's probably was, too." It felt good getting everything out to the one person that could probably call off the charges. If she could convince him, she might be able to save her life.

"Have a seat, Ms. Benton. Trust me, we're about to get to the bottom of this." He picked up the phone and asked someone to join them.

Vanessa prayed he wasn't calling security.

"Ms. Benton, all this is very good. I have to admit, it's more than I expected. When you said you had some evidence, I never expected anything this thorough and detailed. Have you shared this with anyone other than Jane?"

"Yes, Detective Daniels."

The door opened and Brenda walked in. She had a small purse on her shoulder. She closed the door and leaned her back against it.

Vanessa stood. "Brenda." Confused, she turned back to Mr. Steel.

"Come on, have a seat, Ms. Benton. Brenda is here to serve as my witness."

"Witness to what?" Vanessa asked as she sat back down.

He pulled a piece of paper from his desk drawer and slowly pushed it across his desk to her. "To you signing this document stating that you stole the seventy thousand dollars, and to keep yourself out of jail you agree to pay it back. That way I won't have to press charges. And I can erase your name from my list."

The reality of what he said hit Vanessa like a blow to the stomach. He was the thief! She felt sick. The list existed, and she was on it. Just as she'd suspected, she was next to die.

Twenty-two

Two hours later, Eric thought he was wearing Ronnie down.

"No way, man. I didn't take any of that money." Ronnie's voice changed to a high pitch. "I'm not a thief. You can't pin nothing on me."

"How about murder?" Eric said, his voice thick with insinuation and his eyes narrowing with contempt. He didn't believe any more than Vanessa did that Ronnie was capable of murder. But he knew something.

Ronnie's face paled as he forced a smile. When he spoke, his voice crackled and he cleared his throat. His lisp got worse by the hour. "I athed him for help. I wanted to get out of this meth. After we rode around, I carried him back to hith car and I went home. He wath alive when I left him."

"Why didn't you tell the police about meeting him?"

"Becauthe I knew they'd think I killed him. Like you're thinking right now. But I thwear to God I didn't."

"Then who did?"

"Man, I don't know. Maybe he did kill himthelf."

Eric paced the room again. "Maybe you and Ms. Singleton didn't want to share the money with him, so you took him out of the picture. Which one of you pulled the trigger?"

"Man, I told you all I know."

"Harper, you think he'll look good in prison blue?"

Eric sat on the corner of the desk in the room, with his arms crossed.

"Yeah, he'll look real sweet." Harper let out a hearty laugh.

"I think so, too. Maybe you're not out of the closet yet, but it'll be hard to—"

"Okay, man, okay!" Ronnie yelled. "I ain't going to jail for no murder I didn't commit."

"Who killed him, Ronnie? We want to know, and we want to know now!" Harper moved close to him.

"I don't know," Ronnie yelled. "Ask Mr. Steel." He looked down at the floor, shaking his head.

Eric dropped his pen, and sat back. "Harper, it looks like we're going to need another warrant."

When Eric walked out of the interrogation room, an officer was standing outside with Harper. "Got something you might want to take a look at." Harper handed Eric a piece of paper.

"This doesn't look like my warrant."

"It's on the way."

Eric read over the note, then balled it up. He threw the paper in the trash and ran over to his desk. Vince Steel had pressed charges against Vanessa for theft.

He tried her house, then her sister's. No one was home. Then he tried her cell phone. When he couldn't get through, he remembered Vanessa saying she only turned it on in emergency situations. He slammed the phone down. He had to get to her. He'd promised to protect her.

Vanessa sat in Mr. Steel's office so outdone with herself she didn't know what to do. She was cooked. Again she hadn't listened to Eric, but now it was too late. When would she ever learn?

She shook her head. "I'm not signing anything." She slowly stood. "I see what's going on here. It's you. You took that money." She looked at Brenda as she backed away from his desk. "So the rumors about the list weren't just rumors. Was Christopher on the list?"

Mr. Steel gestured toward Brenda.

"Right before yours. But, Vanessa, it didn't have to come to this. You should have let the detectives do their job."

Vanessa shifted when Brenda turned on her, too. She thought about pushing her out of the way and running out of that office, straight to the police station.

"Brenda, how can you do this to me?"

"To you! How come you had to start snooping around? You are definitely more clever than I thought."

"Yeah, well you're not nearly as smart as I thought you were. Brenda, how did you get mixed up in this?" Vanessa walked toward her.

"That's right, Ms. Benton. You should have let the detectives handle the suicide of Christopher Harris. If you had, you'd be sitting behind your desk working right now," Vince broke in.

Vanessa stopped and glared at him. "You killed Christopher?"

"My, my, my. She is clever, isn't she?" He leaned back in his high-back leather chair.

"I told you this wouldn't work. I told you we should have cut our losses with the last one," Brenda added impatiently.

"Shut up." He yanked the paper from his desk and thrust it at Vanessa. "Are you going to sign this or not?"

"What if I don't?" she asked defiantly.

"I cross your name off my list." With his pen he made a big X in the air. A sinister chuckle escaped his lips.

Petrified, she shook her head. "I won't sign it. The police are going to figure out what's going on here." She looked over at her supposed friend, Brenda, still blocking the door.

"I know what you did. You set up the accounts for him, didn't you? You had to. All accounts have to be set up by an account reporter. You set them up, and worked them under Jack's I.D. Then you authorized payment by forging my signature or Christopher's."

Vince reached into his pocket and pulled out his car keys. He stood and tossed them to Brenda. "Take care of this for me. I have work to do."

"But Christopher found out, didn't he?" Vanessa kept talking. "He found out and you killed him." She turned and pointed at Vince Steel.

"Shut up, or you're going to be lying next to him." He gestured to Brenda. "Take her to my car. I'll be right down."

"Oh, no, you don't." Vanessa stepped toward the door, but abruptly stopped.

Brenda held a small handgun. "Don't force me to use it, Vanessa. Because if I have to, I will."

Vanessa backed up. "You won't do that. It'll make too much noise."

"You want to take that chance?" Brenda sneered at her.

Vanessa snorted. "And I thought we were friends."

"But I am your friend. Now, let's walk out of here like the buddies we are, remember?"

Eric weaved through traffic with his arrest warrant in hand. He already had proof that Vince Steel, the director of processing at Brightline, was in debt and padding his expense reports. Mr. Eagan, the company president, had his lawyer watching Vince for the past two months.

Christopher's death had been the third in two years for the small company. That had concerned Mr. Eagan.

Eric swung into the company parking lot with Harper holding on.

"I'll make sure two men stay in the lobby in case we have any trouble," Harper said, righting himself in the seat.

"Don't worry. I don't think he'll give us any trouble. This guy's not a runner. Besides, he has no idea we're on to him."

"He's embezzled over one hundred seventy thousand dollars. He probably figures we'll show up at some point."

"Not if he thinks he's outsmarted us."

They jumped out of the car and Harper went to talk with the cops who'd followed them there. He had two of them stay downstairs, while the other two went with them.

Brenda pushed the button for the elevator and stood next to Vanessa. She held the gun inside her jacket—pointed at Vanessa but out of sight.

Vanessa watched her, unable to believe what was happening. This woman had been in her home. She'd even helped her when Christopher died. "I don't understand. Why are you doing this?"

Brenda flipped her hair out of her face as a small smile formed on her face. "Why do you think?" She never took her eyes from the elevator door.

"For the money? Brenda, don't be stupid. How much do you think he's going to share with you?"

The elevator door open and Brenda gestured for Vanessa to get in. She did.

"Do you know how much I made last year?" Brenda asked from behind her.

"I'm sure he gave you a pretty good raise for helping him, but it doesn't matter. I can't believe you'd risk all that jail time for a little money."

"I'm not just talking raises. I made over one hundred thousand dollars on top of my salary. Not bad for an accounts reporter, huh?"

"Is that all? You killed Christopher over a measly hundred thousand dollars?"

"I didn't kill him. I've never killed anyone, you hear me? I'm in this for the money."

"Why did you pretend to be my friend all that time? Were you guys planning on killing me, too?"

"You know," Brenda laughed, "I bet you drive that detective crazy. You sure as hell talk a lot. Do you shut up long enough to let him make love to you? I bet you don't."

"We're not that close."

"Oh, yeah? Then what was he doing in your bed at three o'clock in the morning the other night—going over Christopher's case?"

Vanessa slowly looked back at her. She saw the corners of Brenda's mouth drop as she realized what she'd just said. "How did you know he was there?"

The elevator door opened on the garage level. Brenda pushed the gun into Vanessa's back. "Walk."

Eric and his team stepped off the elevator on the eighteenth floor. As he walked toward Nikki's desk, he saw her pick up the phone.

"Put it down." He pointed and gave her a keep-your-mouth-shut look.

She froze with the receiver in midair then slowly replaced it.

As the officers approached her, Eric could see her face stricken with fear. He knew he'd be able to catch Vince

Steel unaware. He pointed for one of his men to stay there with her. "We're going to see Mr. Steel. No need in calling him." The three men kept walking until they reached Steel's office.

Eric knocked on the closed door. "Vince Steel, this is Detective Daniels. I'd like to have a word with you."

He got no reply. The blinds on the doors were turned up, so Eric couldn't tell if he was inside or not. He looked at Harper who had his hand on his gun.

Slowly, Eric opened the door. The office was empty. "He's not here. Damn it, he's not here." He hurried out of the office and back to Nikki's desk.

"Where's your boss?"

"I don't know." She shrugged.

Eric looked at his watch. Too early for lunch. "Is he in a meeting or something?"

"No, I don't know where he's at. He was there a few minutes ago. Maybe he's in the men's room or something." She shrugged again.

"We'll just go see about that." He rushed down the hall, headed for the men's room.

"Hello, Officer Daniels" came a young voice from behind him.

Eric turned around to see one of the employees he'd interviewed regarding Christopher Harris's death. He couldn't remember her name, but he recognized the face.

"If you're looking for Vanessa, you just missed her."

"Vanessa!" What the hell was she doing there?

"Yeah, I just saw her and Brenda getting on the elevator."

Eric looked back at Harper.

"I'll notify the guys out front. You catch her, I'll look for Steel." Harper and one of the officers ran off for the men's room.

Eric took the stairs around from the elevator and tried to beat them down. He didn't know if they were leaving the building, or going down to the cafeteria. He just hoped he could catch them before they got away.

He prayed Vanessa wasn't about to get herself killed. Steel and Singleton were in this together. They'd do whatever they had to to keep from going to jail. They proved that when they killed Christopher.

When he reached the first floor, he opened the door and briskly walked down the hall. No sign of them. Assured they weren't on the first floor, he ran back to the stairs. The bottom floor was the garage.

The minute Eric opened the garage door, he saw someone walking across the parking lot. He popped the strap on his gun and crept out into the garage, trying not to be detected. Right away he noticed Vanessa. Brenda walked behind her with a purse on her shoulder.

He tried to get closer before saying anything. When he did, he noticed the way Brenda kept one hand inside her jacket. No doubt, she had a gun. Ahead of them he saw two police officers crouching between parked cars.

Eric jumped out into the open and called out her name, "Vanessa."

When she spun around, Brenda pulled the gun from her jacket and held it to Vanessa's head. The two police officers jumped up from their spots and pointed their guns at Brenda.

"Freeze," Eric yelled. "Brenda, you don't want to do that. Come on, put the gun down."

Vanessa felt the tip on the gun touch her hair and started to freak out. Her legs trembled, and she nearly gagged when her heart rushed up into her throat. She looked into Eric's eyes, wanting to run across the garage to him. But if she did, she could see Brenda shooting her in the back, like she'd seen in so many movies.

"No, you put your gun down," Brenda called back to him.

"We don't want to hurt you."

"We?"

Vanessa felt Brenda move and she looked to her left and saw two more officers in the garage pointing guns at them. The gun at her head began to tremble. She heard Brenda mumble something to herself.

"Brenda, please put the gun down. I'm not going anywhere, and I don't want to see you get hurt," Vanessa pleaded with her.

"Shut up. I told you, you talk too damned much."

The gun pressed against her head harder this time. The metal felt cold and hot at the same time. She heard the quiver in Brenda's voice. She was afraid. She was probably just as afraid as Vanessa.

"Vanessa, are you all right?" Eric asked.

"I'm fine. She won't hurt me."

"You think you know me so well. You don't know anything about me. I'll kill you if I have to."

Eric took a step forward. "Brenda, we know about the money. Come on and put the gun down. Vince is going to get away with everything unless you cooperate. He's not in his office. He's probably already gone and left you to take the rap."

"He's not gone anywhere. This is his car and I've got the keys." She held the keys up and jingled them.

Vanessa looked at the old green Oldsmobile next to them. Now she knew who'd been watching her—Vince Steel. His car had been parked across the street from her house.

A loud noise came from behind Eric as the stairwell door slammed shut and two men stepped out into the parking lot. Brenda jumped and Vanessa screamed as she was pulled to the ground. She saw Eric running toward her with his gun pointed. At the same time, Brenda's hand gripped her hair. What happened to the gun?

The screams and loud commotion caused the men to run back into the stairway. Vanessa reached out and tried to get away from Brenda. Suddenly, her hair was released, and Eric was in front of her as she fell into his arms.

She squeezed her eyes shut as she embraced him and held on for dear life. His arms wrapped around her body and his hand massaged the back of her neck.

"Are you okay? She didn't hurt you, did she?"

Too choked up with fear, all she could do was shake her head. Hot tears rolled down her cheeks, while her heart beat wildly. When she finally got up the courage to turn around, Brenda was handcuffed and leaning again the green Oldsmobile.

A police officer grabbed Brenda and started to walk away. Fear turned into anger. Vanessa couldn't believe Brenda and Mr. Steel had been about to try and kill her. She didn't know what to do, but she couldn't let Mr. Steel get away with this.

"Eric, I heard Mr. Steel tell her he would be right down. They were going to kill me. You've got to get him. He's on his way down here." She held on to Eric's shirt.

Eric reached out and gently stroked her cheek. "What are you doing here anyway?"

"I was waiting for you." She tried to smile.

He snorted, and shook his head. "Come over here." He took Vanessa by the arm and walked over to a waiting officer.

"Sir, do you want us to take her in?" The young officer gestured toward Brenda.

He bit his lip in thought. "No, not just yet. I've got an idea."

A few minutes later, Vanessa watched Brenda sitting in the backseat of Mr. Steel's Oldsmobile, with Eric crouched down on the other side of the car. All the windows were up and it had to be over eighty degrees in that car.

Vanessa squatted a few cars away from the Oldsmobile

with an officer Eric had asked to keep an eye on her for him. She looked down at her shaking hands and took a few deep breaths.

The stairwell door opened again. This time Mr. Steel walked out whistling. With his briefcase in hand, he hustled across the parking lot.

Vanessa's heart beat like a drum in her chest. "Please let Eric be okay," she whispered. She said a silent prayer and tried to remain as still and quiet as she could.

Vince made it halfway across the lot when his pace slowed. He looked at his car and took a few more steps. "Brenda." He stopped and peered at the car, holding his keys in his balled-up fist.

Vanessa shook her head when he called out Brenda's name. It wasn't going to work. He saw Brenda sitting in the backseat and knew something was wrong. He was going to run; she just knew it. She rose a little, to get a better look at him.

The window slowly rolled down in the car and Brenda called out to him. "She's here. Come on."

Vince looked around the lot before proceeding. He stepped closer, with caution this time.

Vanessa watched with bated breath, keeping her fingers crossed that everything would be okay. Once Vince reached the car, Eric would have him. Neither one of them would get away. She got up on the balls of her feet to see a little better, all the while behind the police officer. Suddenly, her foot gave way and she toppled over to the ground, making a thumping sound.

The officer with her reached out to cover her mouth as he helped her back up. The window to the car came down fast this time and Brenda screamed out, "Watch out."

Vince turned and looked in Vanessa's direction before dropping his briefcase and running back toward the stairs.

Eric jumped out and ran around the car, trying to get a good shot at Vince before he reached the garage door. "Freeze!" he yelled.

Before Eric could get a shot off, the door opened and a heavyset woman with two bags on her shoulder walked out. Vince knocked her down in his efforts to get through the doorway. Her bags flew across the parking lot as she hit the ground.

Eric pulled out his two-way and called for backup. The officer with Vanessa started to give chase. Eric yelled for the other officer to watch Brenda.

By this time, Vanessa had already taken the elevator. She pushed the button for the first floor over and over as if the door would close faster. Once the door closed, she leaned again the elevator wall, panting. What the hell was she doing? She wasn't a policewoman. She wasn't trained for this cloak-and-dagger stuff. All she knew was that she couldn't let Steel get away.

The elevator doors opened on the first floor. She stepped off and looked in both directions. Walking toward the revolving door was Vince Steel. She recognized him from behind. He strolled along in an effort not to draw attention to himself. The lobby was pretty crowded. Then she remembered that the building owner was having a book sale. Everyone was combing the lobby for discounted books.

Vanessa pretended to be browsing as she followed Mr. Steel through the lobby. Coming through the building entrance was Mitch, and a few more Brightline managers. She watched Mr. Steel as he greeted them and tried to keep walking. Mitch appeared to be trying to stop him and talk. Outside she could see two police officers headed for the entrance.

She couldn't let him out that door and possibly slip past the policeman. She stepped out into the middle of the lobby and called out his name. "Vince Steel." He looked up at her, waved, but kept walking.

"I know you killed Christopher. You killed him because he found out you stole the money from Brightline." She yelled at the top of her lungs, and drew as much attention to him as she could.

Heads snapped in his direction as everyone looked on in surprise.

Vince stopped short when he saw the officers about to come through the revolving door. He backed up and spun around, trying to find somewhere to go. He quickly took the hall to his left. Before he could reach the door at the end of the hall, two police officers came running through the door. Vince did an about-face.

Vanessa stood there looking at him. Detective Harper, and a few officers ran past her down the hall. Vince raised his hands and leaned against the wall.

He was cuffed and marched back up the hallway. By the time he reached Vanessa, Eric stood behind her with his hand on her shoulder. Vince looked from her to him.

"You don't have anything on me."

"No, and that's why you were running," Eric pointed out.

Mitch Waiters stood behind Eric staring at Vince, his face glazed with shock. A few feet behind him was Nikki Taylor, holding her lunch bag gawking in disbelief.

After Vince was escorted out to the awaiting police car, Vanessa turned to Eric and apologized, "Eric, I'm so sorry, but I just couldn't wait back there and risk him getting away."

He kissed her on the forehead. "I know. You're one of Atlanta's best detectives."

Epilogue

Vanessa walked out of the church and into the sunlight with a heavy heart. Jane would be laid to rest at Forest Lawn Cemetery. Whether her death was related to the Brightline embezzlement case they'd never know. But deep down, Vanessa knew it was. There was no witness to the accident, nor had there been contact with another car.

"Vanessa." A soft feminine voice came from a distance.

When she looked around, to her surprise, Gina Harris was coming toward her.

"Gina, I didn't expect to see you."

She walked up the steps and reached out to hug Vanessa. "Thank you for everything."

Vanessa returned the hug. "You're welcome, but I don't think I did anything really."

"Yes, you did. You didn't give up. I don't think the police felt the same way."

"Gina, the little proof I found would have been nothing if Detective Daniels hadn't listened to me."

"Well, I'll have to thank him, too. And I'm real sorry about your boss."

"So am I."

"I came to pay my respects because she was so nice to me when Christopher passed."

"Yeah, I think after that, the company put her in a bad position. I hope they find out who did this to her."

"Let's just pray to God, and they will."

Two weeks later, Betty dropped by Vanessa's after work to pick up Reggie.

"How's the job?" Vanessa asked.

"It's great. I'm really getting a kick out of working. This Friday, me and some of the girls from work are going to happy hour. Can you keep Reggie for me again?"

Vanessa smiled and nodded. "Anytime."

"And when are you getting back to work?" Betty asked, picking up Reggie's toys from the floor.

"Oh, I don't know. I've got enough money saved to last me about six months, so I'm in no hurry."

"You can't go back to Brightline."

"Betty! Be real. Why would I do that? I've updated my résumé and put out a few feelers. I'm waiting for the right job to come along."

Reggie came running into the room ready to go home.

"Well, once you do, I'll lose my baby-sitter. But you know us Bentons—we're not quitters. Like you told me, get out there and make something happen."

"You know I will. And anytime you want me to baby-sit, just give me a call. I'd do anything for this little guy." Vanessa hugged and kissed Reggie before they left.

"See you Sunday at Mama's for dinner, right?"

"I'll be there."

Vanessa opened the door to let them out, as Eric came up the steps.

Betty looked back at her. "Here comes your Mr. Right."

Vanessa crossed her arms. "I don't know about that.

It's more like he's my ride. The car took longer than I thought."

"Trust me, I know about these things," Betty added as she walked down the steps. She greeted Eric.

Vanessa watched as he briefly talked with Betty before coming in. She never thought she'd be excited to see a policeman again. When he entered, he closed the door behind him and kept walking.

She backed up, smiling and delighted that he was there.

Eric pulled Vanessa into his arms and covered her mouth with his. He kissed her as if he'd been waiting to all day. He backed her over to the wall, never letting go. Once her back was against the wall, he let go.

"Are you glad to see me or what?" she asked, giggling, unable to contain the blush.

"I'm ready to drive to Alabama and pick up your car, but first I've got big news. The case is closed. Vince Steel confessed to murdering Christopher."

"I don't believe he confessed. What happened?"

"He didn't have much of a choice. Your buddy Brenda broke down and told everything. Looks like Ronnie is as innocent as he says he is. Steel wasn't only watching you, he was also watching Ronnie. After he dropped Christopher off, Steel followed him. He thought Ronnie had told Christopher about their scheme. But he didn't have to. Christopher had found that out himself."

"So he knew who was behind everything?"

"Yeah, he'd figured it all out and needed Ronnie's help to blow the lid off everything. However, he didn't get a chance to. Before he made it home, Steel caught up with him. He made him drive back to the club and park in the same spot."

"But why?"

"So when they killed him, everyone would think Ronnie was the last person to see him alive, and possibly his killer. That is, if we didn't buy the suicide."

"Okay, but why didn't they kill Ronnie? He could have told on them."

"Greed. He wanted to process one more transaction, and he needed Ronnie for that. He threatened him pretty good, though. He barely cracked during our interrogation."

Vanessa shook her head. "Wow, this is too much. I can't believe he got Brenda to steal with him."

"Brenda's going away for a long time. Apparently, they've been working this scheme for some time. They worked together at another company before Brightline, and milked them out of money also."

"Eric, I can't believe I sat next to her all that time, and I had no clue about any of this."

"It just goes to show you never really know anyone."

"I knew Christopher wasn't a thief, and thank God you listened to me."

"You made it hard for me not to. But I'll tell you one thing. Because of you, I can add another solved case to my record."

"No." She pressed her index finger against his chest. "Because of me, you don't have to worry about getting involved with anyone on a case again. I'm the best—"

"Vanessa, do you ever shut up?"

"Stick around a while and you'll find out."

"Oh, I plan to. You're stuck with me, baby."

ABOUT THE AUTHOR

Bridget Anderson is a native of Louisville, Kentucky, who now lives in Atlanta, Georgia. She's the author of four other novels—SOUL MATES, RENDEZVOUS, LOST TO LOVE, and REUNITED—and her short story, "Imani," is part of the anthology A KWANZAA KEEPSAKE. When she's not writing or working, she's enjoying her other passion in life—traveling. You can contact Bridget at P.O. Box 76432, Atlanta, Georgia 30358 or via E-mail at Banders319@aol.com.